NASHVILLE CINDERELLA

In Nashville, thousands of talented people hope to make the big time . . . Starstruck Cindy Coin came from Alabama, but still works in Lulu's diner, alongside Tony — who's yet to make his mark. Hank Donno, looking every inch the successful manager, hopes to find his big star — then wide-eyed Katie arrives. And travelling on the Greyhound, Texan Jack just hopes that Nashville is ready for him. Can hopes and dreams be realised? And is romance in the air in Nashville?

JULIA DOUGLAS

NASHVILLE CINDERELLA

Complete and Unabridged

LINFORD
Leicester

First published in Great Britain in 2011

First Linford Edition
published 2012

British Library CIP Data

Douglas, Julia.
Nashville Cinderella. - -
(Linford romance library)
1. Nashville (Tenn.)- -Fiction.
2. Love stories. 3. Large type books.
I. Title II. Series
823.9′2–dc23

ISBN 978–1–4448–0963–3

Published by
F. A. Thorpe (Publishing)
Anstey, Leicestershire

Set by Words & Graphics Ltd.
Anstey, Leicestershire
Printed and bound in Great Britain by
T. J. International Ltd., Padstow, Cornwall

This book is printed on acid-free paper

1

The year was 2005, the place the Ryman Auditorium — the original home of the Grand Ole Opry. They called it the mother church of country music, and back in the 30s it had indeed been a church.

Standing on the edge of the surprisingly narrow sidewalk outside the twin arches of the closed front doors, Cindy Coin tilted her head back as far as it would go. The three tiers of arched windows led her eyes up the dark brown brickwork to a sharp triangle of pitched roof that scratched the grey-blue Nashville sky.

The size of the building was dizzying and so was the sense of history. Early on a chilly Tuesday morning there was barely a soul on the street, but over the past century was there a country singer, from Johnny Cash to Tammy

Wynette, who hadn't stood where she stood now, paying their respects before the altar of country music, before walking around the corner to the stage door? How many millions of fans had worn those smooth dips in the pale grey steps as they swarmed inside to witness the concerts broadcast live on radio station WSM every Saturday night?

Nothing was more overwhelming to Cindy than the fact that she was finally standing here, the stub of a train ticket from Alabama still screwed up in her raincoat pocket, a suitcase in one hand and a guitar case in the other.

A man's voice, low and friendly, spoke just behind her:

'Y'all just got into town?'

Distracted from her reverie, Cindy took a step back. Her heel missed the kerb and she fell backwards into the arms of the most handsome man she'd ever met . . .

* * *

Lulu's was a tiny, old-fashioned diner on Lower Broadway, just around the corner from the Ryman. Everyone had eaten there, from Patsy Cline to Dolly Parton, and even today, in 2010, it was still popular.

Katie knew that from all the interviews she'd read in the country music magazines, and she saw the evidence as soon as she walked in the door. The walls were papered with posters, record sleeves and photographs, all of them signed by country music royalty from A (Eddie Arnold) to Z (Townes Van Zandt).

'It's like walking into a history book!' Katie gushed. Her cowboy boots clomped on the well-scuffed hardwood boards as she turned in a circle, taking it all in.

Hank Donno noted her excitement with the easy smile of a man on his home turf. Indeed, he looked as if he had stepped out of a country-music history book himself. Although his face had an almost baby-like freshness, his vintage, dark pin-stripe suit, that hung loosely from his lanky frame, looked as if it had belonged to his namesake, Hank Williams, the father of country music.

He took off a white Stetson of a similar vintage and smoothed his neatly oiled, retro-styled, light brown hair as he led her to a booth.

'Some of the biggest hits of the last century were written on napkins at these very tables,' Hank drawled. He leaned out of the booth and jerked a thumb at a tiny stage at the dark end of the long, narrow room. 'Kitty Wells, the first gal singer to sell a million copies of a country single, sang on that very spot.'

'Wow!' Katie was impressed if secretly just a little disappointed as well. Having dreamed so long of the day she'd finally get to Nashville, she'd hoped she might see Reba McEntire or Dolly shooting the breeze in one of the other booths, or a couple of top songwriters swapping rhymes on stools in front of the long, dark wood bar.

This morning, though, as the sun slanted in dusty shafts between the half-height café curtains and the canopy that hung over the sidewalk outside, the place was empty.

Hank seemed to read her mind.

''Course, the big stars don't come down town so much any more. These days, it's mainly tourists.'

A brunette waitress in a pink gingham uniform skipped over to their booth with a coffee-pot in her hand almost as soon as they sat down.

'Want some drip, Hank?'

'Thanks, Cindy.' Hank turned over one of the cups waiting upside-down atop their saucers on the check tablecloth, and Katie did likewise. When Cindy had filled them up with steaming, black filter coffee, Hank ordered ham, eggs and pancakes for both of them.

'You've got to have the pancakes at Lulu's!'

'Just like in the song!' Katie beamed back.

On cue, Cindy began to sing in a fine country contralto.

' . . . and then we'll have some pancakes at Lu-hoo-lu's café.'

As the waitress turned on her pink-heeled shoe and skipped back towards the kitchen, Hank watched her with a fond smile.

'That's Cindy Coin, one of the sweetest songbirds in Music City.' He shook his head, regretfully. 'She's been here five years now, and still ain't got a record deal. Sadly, she's not the only one. You know what they say about Nashville, don't ya? If you want to meet a great singer, just holler 'Waiter!' But that's where I can help you, Katie Carnegie.'

As Cindy went into the tiny, white-tiled kitchen Tony Kaplasky, the short order cook, was peering through a crack in the door. Cindy shooed him back into the kitchen.

'I was going to say it looks like Hank's found a new girl singer,' Cindy said, 'but I see you've already had an eyeful.'

Tony, a pink-cheeked, roly-poly figure who looked like the Pillsbury Dough-boy in his white chef's jacket and check trousers, was already back at the crack in the door, his face as dreamy as a 14-year-old girl swooning over a picture of Elvis.

'If she sings half as good as she looks, she's going straight to the top.' He sighed.

'Come away from there!' Cindy chastised him. 'And get busy cookin' this here order.'

Her tone was playful, however, and Tony took it in good part. Cindy loved Tony about as much as she loved anyone in the whole world. In fact, sometimes she felt like he was the only person she had in the whole world. They shared a house in East Nashville, the cheap side of town where all the aspiring singers and musicians lived. It was a strictly best-of-friends arrangement, and neither of them had ever thought for one second that it would be anything else. Tony was the younger brother Cindy never had, and she was the older sister he'd never had, even though there was barely a year between them. Sometimes she thought he was more like one of her girlfriends than a guy.

As soon as Tony moved away to break some eggs on the hotplate, she took his place at the crack in the door, wishing she were close enough to eavesdrop on what Hank and his pretty blonde companion were saying. She couldn't see Hank from this angle, but she could see the girl, her heart-shaped face and slender neck surrounded by cascading blonde curls that shone in the shafts of sunlight slanting through the windows. Her rosebud lips were parted slightly and her incredibly bright eyes were wide and impressed, clearly taking in everything Hank was saying.

Well, Cindy knew how easy it was to believe that long, tall man in the vintage threads. She'd sat where Cutie Pie was now, listening to that smooth-talking son of a gun tell her he was gonna make her a big, big star. She'd believed plenty of other things he'd said, too! Being a charitable kind of girl, she honestly reckoned he believed half the stuff he promised. The thing with Hank was, it was always what he was 'gonna' do. He was gonna be a song publisher; he was gonna be a manager. He was gonna do a lot of things, was Hank!

He was gonna call you, Cindy remembered, a bit more sadly. But then, who knew? If this girl was his new discovery, Hank, the aspiring big shot manager, might finally be about to hit the jackpot.

Although it gave Cindy just the teeniest twinge of jealousy to admit it, Tony was right about the girl. If she only sang half as good as she looked, the record companies were going to fall over themselves to sign her up. Duded up in that crazy fringed cowgirl suit of hers, she already looked a star.

'What's happening?' Tony hissed behind her, struggling to see.

'Shh!' She elbowed him. Then, 'He's

handing her a contract! She's signing it!'

'If that's a management deal, he's got it made!'

She spun round.

'You know what this means, don't you?'

The chef looked at her blankly.

'She's going to need songs! This is your chance to pitch her a hit before every other songwriter in town. Come on, what have you got that would suit a girl like that?'

Tony screwed up his face in thought.

'How about, I'm In the Mood For A Cheatin' Song?'

'No, no, no. That's far too old for her. She only looks about 21. What have you got that would suit a gal her age?'

Tony thought some more, then remembered one he'd written just the week before.

'How about, I Want Your Body, Cowboy?'

Cindy remembered him playing it for her, on his acoustic guitar in their living room — a real sassy, Shania Twain type of song. It wasn't something Cindy would be able to sing, she knew — she was more of a torch song singer. But for the photogenic girl in the booth with Hank, it could be ideal.

'That's perfect!' she enthused.

'You think?' Tony beamed at her.

She gave him a curious look.

'How'd you come to write a girly song like that anyhow?'

Tony looked momentarily caught out. But, before he could answer, a high pitched shriek of horror almost blew the kitchen door in. Cindy and Tony ran for the door.

'Singing lessons?' Katie hollered in a voice they would have heard at Willie Nelson's house — and that was in Texas.

Hank put up his palms, like train buffers, to placate her.

'Now, I'm not saying you ain't got a great natural talent, Katie. But you're young, untrained and inexperienced. Before I put you in front of the major labels I think you need to spend just a little time with someone like Cindy. Just to learn a few tricks of the trade.'

Turning her outrage down to a barely controlled simmer, Katie studied him through eyes narrowed like a rattlesnake's.

She had to admit he stood up to the scrutiny well. Leaning back in a suit cut from cloth as old as the upholstered back of the booth seat, looking exactly like one of the old time country music legends whose black and white pictures lined the walls, his body language was relaxed and laid back, completely unflustered by her outburst.

Eventually, he lifted his eyebrows slightly, as if to say, 'Trust me.'

Cindy, watching from the kitchen door, couldn't see Hank, who was hidden by the back of his booth seat, but she could tell from Katie's grudgingly mollified expression exactly the kind of look he was giving her. It was one that had worked on Cindy plenty of times before.

* * *

Hank drove Katie over to Cindy and Tony's house right after they got back from the day shift at Lulu's. Tony bustled around their little living room, tidying up like a housewife caught out by an unexpected visitor. As he huffed and puffed, picking up guitars, CD cases and used mugs, Cindy stood at the window and watched Hank's big, black 1957 Chevrolet pull up outside.

The last of the late afternoon sun gleamed like a lipstick smudge on the flattened dome of the car's roof and the fat bull nose of the hood, the distinctive low burble of the antique V8 engine stirring up memories in Cindy like long-settled mud swirling around at the bottom of a creek as a long, sleek, dangerous-looking pike swam by. She remembered the shiny, brittle feel of the Chevy's faded mint-green leather upholstery, worn into permanent rump-shaped dents by half a century of use.

She remembered, too, the distinctive

rough caress of the wool in those fifty-year-old suits of Hank's. Modern fabrics just didn't feel the same, or smell the same. With the rough wool on her cheek and the lapel against her nose, they never lost that faint but seductive smell of history. It was a scent she'd never smelled anywhere else and which she'd never forget.

It was strange how wearing the clothes of men who were probably long dead only made Hank look more youthful. In the diner earlier he hadn't looked a day older than he had the day she'd fallen off a kerb and into his arms outside the Ryman Auditorium. After five years of waiting tables, singing in late-night bars and pinning her hopes on auditions for record deals that never happened, Cindy doubted she herself looked fresh-faced. Then again, she doubted she'd ever looked as young as the angel-featured Katie Carnegie.

As she watched from the window, Hank spotted her and gave her a wave and a little wink, but didn't climb out of the car. Cindy waved back, but he'd already turned away towards Katie as she got out of the passenger door, then opened the back door and took her guitar case from the back seat. Katie slammed the door with a rattly clunk that was so familiar it gave Cindy's heart a little start. Then Hank made the engine burble a little louder and she watched the black tail fins slide away from the kerb, the way she'd watched them so many times before. The last thing she saw, before the car disappeared from view, was Hank's pinstriped arm hanging languidly out the open driver's window, one finger trailing through the air like he was James Dean.

Katie came into the house with her arms folded defensively around her guitar case, which was clasped upright like a shield against her belly.

Cindy felt for her. She remembered what it was like to arrive alone in Nashville. To be told, on your first day, that you needed singing lessons was more than anyone deserved. She wasn't surprised Hank had delivered the singer and driven off immediately. She could bet relations between Hank and Katie had remained pretty frosty all day.

The look in Katie's eyes certainly suggested she'd brought plenty of attitude with her, although she was holding it all in. Cindy however was determined to be nice. Hank hadn't had to use too much charm to persuade her to give Katie some vocal tuition — free of charge, of course. He could still twist her around his little finger. But whatever there had been between her and Hank was well and truly in the past. They'd both agreed that, hadn't they? Water under the bridge, and good friends again. She didn't begrudge Hank finding a new young girlfriend, even if she'd never allowed herself to fall for someone new herself.

Besides, for all she knew, Hank's interest in Katie was purely professional. He knew lots of singers. That was his job, as far as he ever had what most people would call a job.

As for Cindy's feelings towards Katie, well, Katie was a singer, a Music City hopeful just the same as Cindy, Tony and just about everyone else they knew in town. They were all in this together, all chasing the same dream against the same impossible odds. Cindy would offer any help she could give her, even if a sinking feeling in her stomach told her that Katie might be one of those lucky ones for whom the dream came true, while Cindy was beginning to face the possibility that she might herself end up as one of the many who tried and failed.

She was glad Tony was home. She had a feeling that, had she been on her own, Katie's defensiveness would have proved insurmountable, but Tony's playful-puppy persona was always a good ice-breaker. He was so unthreatening girls always relaxed in his company.

'So,' Cindy said briskly once Tony had fixed them some coffee and a snack. 'How about you start by singing us something, and we'll just take it from there?'

Katie shrugged, and unclicked the clasps on her guitar case. She stood up, as if it would give her more confidence, and as she began to strum, Cindy was aware once more of her star quality, despite her obvious nervousness. She'd chosen a recent song by Lee Ann Womack that was so traditional it could have come from the mid-70s' repertoire of Tammy Wynette. The song suited Katie's fringed skirt and two-tone buckskin jacket, even though, Cindy reflected with an inward smile, absolutely no-one in Nashville wore that old-fashioned stuff anymore. None of the women, anyway. The guys, like Alan Jackson and George Strait, still clung on to their cowboy hats. Then, too, there was Hank, with his vintage suits from the 40s and 50s.

She had to stop thinking about Hank and concentrate on Katie's singing. She wasn't sure why he'd got so under her skin tonight. For years now, she'd hardly given him a second thought, even though, in a music community as small and close-knit as Nashville, you were never far from a door that Hank's square-jawed face might appear in at any moment.

Katie finished the song with a final twang on her guitar and Tony, watching from the couch, gave a whoop and holler of approval.

Cindy clapped, too.

'That was real good!'

Katie grinned with a mixture of relief and smugness.

'See? I told Hank I didn't need no singing lessons!'

Cindy put her head on one side.

'Well, I can see where Hank thought you might be able to build on what you've got. Take that bit where you go up to the bridge. Why don't you try it like this?'

She picked up a spare guitar and sang a couple of lines to demonstrate.

Katie listened, then put her guitar in her case.

'Well, I'm just gonna pack up and go back to Florida, because if that's how well the waitresses sing, y'all don't need me in this town! How on earth do you do that?' she asked, laughing.

'It's just technique and practise,' Cindy said modestly. 'You'll pick it up no problem.'

'Do you think so?'

For the next hour, Cindy taught Katie some basic vocal exercises while Tony helped out, playing guitar chords to keep them on key. Katie was a quick learner and because she could hear herself improving, she soon got over her resentment at having to learn.

By the time Cindy judged they'd done enough work for one evening, the two women were getting on well enough to chat easily.

Katie, it turned out, had grown up in the Everglades. Her rich folks hated her love of country music, and wanted to marry her off to the son of the local senator. Katie, never much liking being told what to do, packed her guitar, caught a cab to Miami and got a job singing in the lounge of a beachfront hotel. Hank happened to be staying there on vacation and told her he was a talent scout for all the big record companies in Nashville.

'So, are you and Hank . . . ?'

'No way!' Katie giggled explosively.

For some reason, Cindy felt better about that, although she wondered why Katie found the idea so funny. She guessed new young kids in town weren't as easily impressed by smooth-talking charmers like Hank as they used to be!

'Actually,' Katie said shyly, 'I wondered if you and Hank were . . . ?'

'No way!' Cindy echoed. With a soft smile, she confided, 'Well, a long time ago.'

'He talks about you a lot.'

'He does?'

'He's always saying what a great

singer you are, and how well-respected around town. If you'll excuse me being personal, seeing as you are such a great singer I was wondering how come Hank wasn't able to get you a record deal?'

Cindy looked away while she considered her response. She didn't want to be bitter and start putting Hank down. Nor did she want to disillusion Katie about the tough reality of the music business.

At length, she spoke in a level tone.

'Things aren't always as easy and straightforward as Hank can make them sound.' To break what could have become a downbeat mood, she added with a sudden mischievous smile, 'Do you know his real name's not even Hank?'

'Really?' She giggled, and again Cindy was aware how lovely she was.

'Honest. It's Gordon!'

'No way!' Both women laughed like schoolgirls.

Tony came through from the kitchen

with a tray of home-baked cookies and maple syrup. Feeding other people and feeding himself were his two favourite pastimes . . . after writing country songs.

'Is Hank picking you up later?' Tony asked Katie.

'No, he gave me money to catch a cab. I'm staying at the Holiday Inn, although I need to find somewhere more permanent — and cheaper.'

'Why don't you stay here? We have a spare room, haven't we, Cindy?'

She shot Tony a look. She liked Katie, but having her move in would mean seeing an awful lot more of Hank, and she wasn't sure that was what she wanted just at the moment.

'That would be so cool!' Katie was enthusing. 'You can give me singing lessons and show me around town!'

'Our other house-mate, Marcia, has just gone on tour as a backing singer to a famous artist.' Cindy named him. 'I guess you could have her room until she gets back.'

'That's agreed then!' Tony picked up a guitar. 'Now, listen to this, Katie. I've got this song I think would suit you so much!'

2

The converted Greyhound bus hammered westward on Highway 54, the gleaming silver bodywork leaning on its springs as it barrelled around a wide curve. The lights from its side windows were an orange streak against the blood-red sunset, and fiddle-led country music tumbled out of the vents in its wake. At a steering wheel the size of a ship's, Gator, the driver, had a CB radio microphone in one hand.

'Breaker 1-9, this is the Music Man. Y'all passed any speed traps? Come on, come on.'

'That's a negatory, good buddy,' came the crackly voice of a friendly trucker four or five miles ahead. 'You're clear all the way to Twang Town.'

As the headlights picked out a sign flashing by on the roadside, Gator honked the horn.

'Nashville here we come!' he hollered. Inside the bus half a dozen musicians, playing cards or toying with guitars, raised their voices in a rousing chorus of whoops, hollers and 'Yee-haa's!' Only one man didn't join the chorus — the man whose name was emblazoned in three-foot-tall letters along the aluminium sides of the bus. The name of Texan Jack Dallas.

Texan Jack — Tex to his buddies — was stretched out across the back seat of the bus, his black leather trousers and heavy motorcycle boots sticking out from beneath a black poncho that enveloped his body like a shroud. A black Stetson was pulled down completely over his face. In one hand he held a bottle of beer propped on his belly. His other hand hung off the side of the seat and rested, lovingly, on a guitar beside him.

'You ready for Nashville, Tex?' Gator hollered down the bus.

Tex used the lip of his beer bottle to lift the brim of his hat, revealing a face so pale and perfectly sculptured that Michelangelo might have carved it. He blinked at the light, then cracked a grin and said in a low, low drawl, 'I hope Nashville is ready for Texan Jack!'

* * *

Lower Broadway was teaming with tourists on a Friday night, all of them hoping to get a taste of grass-roots Nashville from the wannabe country stars playing for tips in the bars and clubs that lined the thoroughfare. Real stars were not to be glimpsed, although Willie Nelson's tour bus, the Honeysuckle Rose, was parked a little way down the block, raising the hopes of the holidaymakers who recognised it.

A Closed For Private Party notice swung inside the glass door of Lulu's. Inside, the crowd was packed in tightly. Cindy and Tony were jammed into a corner by the sidewalk end of the bar, where they could get served and where they'd also be able to kneel up on the barstools and get a get a clear view of the tiny stage. Both had called in every favour they had to make sure they were off duty, and Cindy had put on a tight-fitting, sparkly blue knee-length dress. Diamond earrings peeped from neatly bobbed hair that shone like a chestnut. This was the sort of crowd where it paid to look like a star-in-waiting, as Hank had always told her. Multi-national record executives, tour agents, magazine editors . . .

'The entire music business is in here!' she squealed at Tony above the din of conversation.

As if to confirm her words, she spun around at the sound of a soft, sweet voice that was instantly recognisable.

'Hi, Cindy!'

'Oh, my!' She hugged the country legend like a favourite grandpa, burying her face in the long hair that hung from a centre parting all the way down to his waist. 'I didn't know you were in town!'

'Just got in, and wanted to see this new superstar everybody's talkin' about. Speaking of which, Cindy, have you got your record deal yet?'

Cindy pulled a face, and the star looked sympathetic.

'Keep going and it will happen,' he advised her. 'Sometimes all it takes is the right song. Tony will write one for you, won't you, Tony? Just remember, it all comes down to the song. Excuse me, now. I think I just saw someone I need to talk to over there.'

Cindy watched the diminutive superstar walk away through the crowd, which seemed to part before him, like the Red Sea.

'Look at that,' Cindy said to Tony. 'The greatest country singer that ever lived, and he's still the sweetest guy in the world.'

At that moment, the room lights went down and the tiny stage at the far end of the diner lit up. Cindy hitched up her skirt and leaned on Tony as she climbed on to her knees on her barstool. Tony quickly scrambled into a similar position beside her, just in time to see a lean-faced man with thinning sandy hair shuffle up to the microphone in an expensive suit so crumpled he might have been sleeping in it. Troy Tillman, record producer and record company head, so fabulously rich and successful he could afford to look a permanently distracted mess! Using an upturned palm to shield his eyes from a row of lights that was almost touching his head, he tapped the microphone like he'd never seen one before.

'Ladies and gentlemen, I am so pleased to see so many of you here tonight, in this most historic of venues, to witness a new chapter in country music being written before your very eyes. Please give a big 'Howdy!' to our newest signing, who's also gonna be the next big country music superstar — Miss Katie Carnegie!'

There was no room on the tiny stage for a band, so Hank, stationed beside the stage, put on a backing track and turned the volume up to max. As the thunderous intro to I Want Your Body,

Cowboy shook the posters and photos that covered the walls, Cindy and Tony gripped each other, both of them biting their lower lip and tears erupting simultaneously from the corners of their eyes. Tony had waited for this moment since he'd heard his first Randy Travis record at the tender age of five, and Cindy was unspeakably proud of him.

At the far end of the diner, Hank opened the dressing-room door and Katie took the two steps on to the stage, reaching the microphone just in time to start singing. She was wearing a sparkly silver mini-dress and carrying a golden guitar that was so mirrored it sent blinding flashes of reflection zipping around Lulu's like laser beams. To Cindy's eyes she looked absolutely perfect, like a Barbie doll wrapped in cellophane. She sounded gorgeous, too, employing all the vocal phrasing Cindy had spent so many hours schooling her in. Seeing all their work paying off, on top of the pride she felt in Tony for writing the song, made Cindy feel she was going to just burst.

Cindy didn't hear the door from the street open behind her, the jangling of the bell above it completely drowned by the music. But she did notice a leather-clad, raven-haired, pale-featured man making his way slowly but inexorably through the crowd towards the front. She did a double take, and then just plain stared. The guy looked like a young Elvis and a young Johnny Cash rolled into one.

Tony's jaw flopped on to Cindy's shoulder.

'Who is that?' he breathed in Cindy's ear.

The place was so tightly packed it should have been impossible for the leather-clad, pale-faced stranger to move through it. But the crowd seemed to open up before him as if by magic. Without breaking his stride or wavering in direction, he cut through it like a hot knife through butter until he was standing directly in front of the stage, staring at Katie. From her vantage point on her barstool, Cindy saw Katie do the same sort of double take she had herself, almost missing a line of the song. She swiftly recovered, but from that point sang the song directly and exclusively to the newcomer as if they were the only ones in the room.

When Katie's brief showcase was over, and Hank had shooed her off stage into the dressing-room, the room erupted into volcanic applause. Cindy slid off her barstool and grabbed Tony's hand.

'Let's get over there!'

Everyone was moving in the same direction, but Cindy and Tony used their elbows like bargain-hunters in a New Year sale to reach the front. Beside the tiny stage were three doors. The first led to the rest rooms, the one in the back wall was a fire-escape door that led to an alley, and the door squashed between them led to the tiny dressing-room. Hank was guarding the door, keeping everyone out while simultaneously cutting noisy, tough-talking deals with a casino chain owner and a tour promoter. With a tall white Stetson adding to his height, he looked even more imposing than normal.

Without breaking off from either of the two conversations he was having, except to shout 'No!' at a photographer who was trying to get into the dressing-room, he opened the door just long enough for Cindy and Tony to slip inside before slamming it shut again. The room was tiny, packed and as hot as an oven. Katie was sitting on the dressing-table in her sparkly silver dress, with her back to a mirror surrounded by light bulbs, her long legs crossed and one stiletto heel propped on a cheap plastic chair. The pale-featured stranger in black leather was standing so close to her they looked like lovers. Troy Tillman and a couple of record company suits were hovering in attendance.

'Cindy!' Katie squealed, leaning out to hug her friend's neck. 'Meet Tex.

Tex, this is my best friend in the whole of Nashville — Cindy Coin!'

Tex grinned at Cindy.

'Well, I'm pleased to meet you, baby doll.'

Simultaneously stunned by the stranger's handsomeness and repulsed by the arrogance that radiated from every pore of him, Cindy heard herself say, stupidly, 'Likewise . . . Tex?'

'Texan Jack Dallas,' he introduced himself. 'And don't apologise for not knowin'. Back home in Texas they treat me like some kind of cult hero, but up here in Nashville, I guess there ain't but nobody even knows my name!'

He flashed a switchblade grin at the record company people who laughed, nervously. All except Troy Tillman, who barely looked up from a palmtop computer he was tapping away on.

'That's about to change, Tex,' he muttered. 'This time next year you'll be national. Bigger than Garth Brooks was!'

'Tex just came into town to sign a

record deal,' Katie explained. 'And guess what? We're on the same record label!'

She reached out to hug Tony.

'This is my other best friend, Tex. Tony, who wrote my song!'

By this point, Cindy had sized Tex up as an obnoxious, swaggering high-school bully, and if anyone in the room looked like the sort of kid Tex would have bullied in school it was the roly-poly, girly-featured Tony. But when Tex leaned across Katie's lap to shake Tony's hand, Cindy saw suddenly a new side to the leather-clad newcomer. The Texan looked deeply interested, and almost humbled.

'No kidding?' he drawled. 'That's a good song, buddy.'

Tony blushed.

'Oh, it's just a ditty . . . '

'Don't knock it,' Tex insisted, 'A fun song's as hard to write as a sad song, and that's a quality lyric. One of the reasons I wanted to come to Nashville was to see how you guys write. How about you and me getting together to write something?'

Tony was dumbstruck, but before he found his voice the door opened to admit a blast of noise from the diner and Hank stuck his Stetson-topped head into the room.

'Limo's here, Katie. We're going out the back door. Cindy, Tony — y'all coming with us?'

He threw the door open and shielded them from the crowding mob while Katie, Cindy and Tony ran the couple of steps from the dressing-room to the fire-door in the back of the diner. Tex followed them through and Hank brought up the rear, Katie's guitar case in his hand, and closed the door behind them.

After the sweltering crush of the diner, the night air of the dark back alley hit them like a blast of ice-cold air-conditioning. Exhilarated and laughing, they half skipped, half ran towards a white stretch Hummer limo that was parked across the mouth of the alley, its door open invitingly. Hank shooed Cindy into the pink-lit interior, then blocked Katie and Tex as a press photographer stepped from the shadows.

'Smile, guys!'

With grins already plastered across their faces, Katie hugged Tex's snake-like waist while he clasped an arm around her slender shoulders. The photographer's camera flashed four or five times, then Hank whisked the singers into the limo.

* * *

The drive home was short, and the loud rumble of the Hummer's diesel engine reminded Cindy of the bus she caught each day. But the journey had never been more fun than it was, sandwiched between Tony and Hank on the long, sofa-like seats beneath a mirrored ceiling, as they all tried not to spill their complimentary glasses of champagne on the deep-pile carpet and disco lights flashed above a sound system playing

Katie's recording of I Want Your Body, Cowboy at full blast.

As they all fell about in the party-like atmosphere, high on the events of the evening so far, Cindy took the opportunity to link her arm through Hank's and briefly nuzzle her face against his shoulder, refamiliarising herself with the rough grain of the wool on her cheek and that delicious smell that only Hank's 50-year-old vintage suits possessed.

In the disorientating nightclub lighting, which was flashing from pink to blue to green and falling into inky black darkness in between, she doubted he even noticed. He was trying to cut a deal of some kind with Tex, who in turn was more interested in trying to give Katie a playful squeeze and a kiss on the neck. Meanwhile, Tony leaned full-length across Cindy's lap and Hank's in his efforts to snaffle a complimentary doughnut from a tray on the limo's central coffee table.

For Cindy, though, that brief reconnection with Hank's suit and all the memories it brought back was blissful. As the Hummer stopped and she opened her eyes, she wondered if she imagined it or whether he held her gaze, briefly before moving to open the door. It was hard to tell.

As the music spilling from the limo announced to the neighbours their return home — though late-night blasts of country music were more usual than not in a street where every other house was rented by musicians — Katie tottered out of the car clutching a bottle of champagne.

Cindy came next, carrying Katie's guitar case, and Tony brought up the rear, clutching the tray of doughnuts, a box of chocolates and whatever other edible goodies had been included in the limo's hire charge. Tex tried to join them on the sidewalk, but Hank blocked his exit from the car.

'Not tonight, Romeo. Ladies need their sleep.'

'I'm not sleepy!' Katie piped up.

'Me neither!' Cindy joined in.

But Hank was stern.

'Tomorrow's a work day, Katie. Get an early one.'

After some final goodbyes, Hank waved them off towards their house and climbed back into the limo with Tex. He pulled the door closed and signalled the chauffeur to drive on.

As the red tail lights of the Hummer turned out of the end of the street and the bus-like sound of the engine faded into the distance, Katie and Cindy piled through their front door, giggling about Texan Jack.

'I saw him first!' Katie squealed.

'No, you didn't, I did, and Tony's a witness to that!' Cindy joked.

Of course, she wasn't really interested in Tex, and wouldn't in a million years have expected a guy like that to be interested in her. Still, his striking looks and charisma were still exciting and gossip-worthy in that completely unattainable way that, say, a brief unexpected meeting with Brad Pitt would keep one in excitable conversations for a good while. That Tex actually seemed more than interested in Katie only added to the amusement.

'By the way, did you get his phone number?'

Katie stopped dead, with her jaw hanging open.

'Do you know, in all the confusion, I didn't! I didn't even give him mine!'

'I got it!' Tony triumphantly waved a napkin with squiggled figures on it. 'He's coming over tomorrow to write a song with me!'

3

Tony was lucky the next morning. He was on the evening shift at Lulu's and got to lie in. Cindy yawned as she struggled in to work. After all the excitement, it had ended up being a late night. Luckily, mornings tended to be slow. In the mid-morning lull between breakfast and lunch, Cindy found herself alone in the diner.

She was just leaning on the bar, having a restorative cup of black java, when the bell jangled and in walked Hank. He came over to the bar and hauled himself up on to one of the stools. Cindy usually always put on a little make-up for work, but as Hank came close, she was briefly conscious that she hadn't made much effort with her face this morning, and that she probably looked a little tired.

Still, that was the upside of being just

good friends — you didn't have to worry so much about things like that.

With a wry inward smile she remembered what she used to be like before a date with Hank — standing in front of the mirror trying on the umpteenth dress, the rest strewn on the bed behind her.

Asking Tony, 'Now, come on, be honest, do you really think this colour suits me?' while even Tony, who could stand more clothes-talk than most guys, had rolled his eyes and pretended to fall into a coma. Then there were all those oh-my-gosh-what-do-I-look-like? moments, when she bumped into Hank unexpectedly.

Oh my gosh, the wind's making my hair look like a dead crow! Oh my gosh, is there chocolate on my teeth? Oh my gosh, I've just eaten anchovies and garlic! It hadn't helped that Hank always looked immaculate. She had been paranoid about getting emotional and letting mascara run on to those precious vintage suits of his.

This morning, he was as sharply dressed as ever, though she noticed with some satisfaction that his generally baby-fresh complexion looked a little paler than usual, and that there was the hint of dark shadows beneath eyes that looked a little crumpled at the edges. He looked as though he'd given Tex a good tour of Nashville's late-night drinking spots. Well, Hank knew every one of them.

The sleepy-eyed, just-lifted-his-head-from-the-pillow look didn't make him any less attractive, she decided wistfully.

'Drip?' Cindy asked, although she never needed to.

Hank gave her that little wink and tilt of the head with a slow carefulness that confirmed her suspicion that he was a little hungover. A small smile played faintly above his shovel-square jaw.

Cindy reached for the always steaming coffee jug and poured him one. He liked it black, same as she did.

'I thought you were supposed to be over Troy's office with Katie, going through songs for her album?'

'Coffee's better here.' He grinned. 'Also, after a night on the town with Tex, loud music's not really what I want to hear right now!'

'What time did you roll in?'

He took off his white Stetson and laid it on the bar.

'I dropped out of the race about 2 a.m. What time Tex got back to his bus, or where he wound up in the meantime, I have no idea.'

They exchanged the comfortable smiles of people who knew each other intimately, but who were not so closely connected that they had any right or cause to question or recriminate with one another about who was where, with whom or doing what at 2am! All those old arguments had been put behind them and, in that respect, Cindy had to admit there was something a lot less stressful about this just-good-friends business.

She'd never enjoyed hating Hank, but if you got too close to a guy like Hank it was easy to end up feeling that way so often that anger and disillusionment was just about all you ended up with. That was why she had ended it.

She never wanted to go back to hating Hank like that. There were lots of things she missed about being in love with him, and, lately, she'd found herself missing them so much she sometimes couldn't sleep at night. But at least from this distance she was able to see him as a friend most of the time.

She smoothed her silky chestnut bob and leaned on the bar so she could take a good look at him.

'Well, Hank,' she said, proudly. 'I guess you finally hit the jackpot.'

His grey-green eyes met hers and she saw a twinkle of satisfaction in them. Then he shrugged.

'Believe me, Cindy, the work ain't started yet. Last night's little launch party was just the beginning. Turning Katie's song into a hit, let alone building a career, is gonna be a whole other matter.'

'You got her a record deal, though. You're a bona fide manager now, just like you always wanted to be.'

She saw his eyes soften and his whole face warm.

'It's been a long uphill climb, Cindy Coin. Took years just to get to the point where someone like Troy Tillman would even answer the phone to someone like me.'

'Don't I know it?' Cindy sighed.

Hank gave her a sympathetic look.

'It'll happen for you, too, Cindy.'

'That's what someone told me last night. Trouble is, I remember him telling me the same thing last time I bumped into him — about this same time last year.'

'That's just the way it is in this town. Look at Tony — tryin', tryin', tryin' to get a song cut. One day Katie walks into town. Suddenly it's the right singer, right song, and now it looks like he's gonna have a number one hit!'

Hank unfolded a copy of that morning's Tennessean, which he'd brought in with him. On the front page was a picture of Katie and Texan Jack cuddled up in the alley last night. The headline said, Country music's Newest Golden Couple.

Cindy had seen it already, and felt a little pang of envy despite herself, knowing she'd been just a few feet away when the photo was taken yet completely out of the picture, in more ways than one.

'Look great together, don't they? I'm thinking maybe I can get some kind of Faith Hill and Tim McGraw thing going with these two. Joint tours, duets . . . ' His voice became more excited as he shrugged off his hangover and began outlining his plans.

Cindy knew he wasn't really talking to her, however. His eyes on the front page, he was going off into his own world. Same old Hank, she thought, always full of plans, always talking about what he was 'gonna do' . . . Only difference was, this time he maybe really would do it. But with Katie as the object of his ambitions when, once, it would have been Cindy.

As she leaned on the bar and gazed past him at one of the empty booths, with its backdrop of country legends pinned to the wall, she found herself tuning out, not even hearing what he was saying. Hank was doing well, Katie was doing well, Tony was doing well. She didn't begrudge any of them the success they seemed poised on the brink of. They'd all worked hard, and they all deserved it.

Still, as she leaned on the bar in her pink gingham waitress uniform and eased a foot out of one of the pink high heels that was rubbing her heel and cramping her toe, she couldn't help feeling like a Nashville Cinderella, working the bar at Lulu's while everyone else went to the ball.

Even her other housemate, Marcia, had phoned to say she wasn't coming home. She'd had a whirlwind romance with a bass player and they were getting married in the fall.

To think Cindy had once thought

there might be wedding bells for her and Hank. In her mind, she'd had the dress made, booked the church and even picked the hymns!

She glanced at him, still making his plans for Katie's career. His mind was so far in the future she doubted he ever gave a thought to the past. He'd moved on long ago.

* * *

Texan Jack rode over to East Nashville on the white and chrome Harley Davidson motorcycle he kept strapped to a rack on the back of his tour bus. He was dressed from head to toe in black leather, his eyes hidden by shades as black and impenetrable as those Arnold Schwarzenegger wore in The Terminator. A guitar case was slung across his back like a rifle.

Tony watched from his living room window as the big bike pulled up outside. The whole house seemed to throb in time with the deep, raspy chug of the engine. The noise died with a coughing metallic clatter as Tex turned the key and rocked the bike back on to its stand with a creak.

He hung his helmet on the handlebar, stretched stiffly and rubbed his neck wearily.

Tony eyed him nervously. Happiest around girls, ultra-manly guys like Tex scared him, and he wished Cindy or Katie were home to lighten the atmosphere. Still, Tex had been nice about his song last night.

He opened the door while Tex's fist was still raised, about to knock.

'I'm just getting some pizza out of the oven, would you like some?' he said in a single breath.

With his eyes hidden by the shades, the rest of Tex's face looked about as healthy as a ghost. But he cracked a smile as he replied in a voice as low and gravelly as the seabed.

'Sounds good — and about three gallons of strong black coffee if you've got it?'

'Coming right up!'

Tex followed Tony into the kitchen. He perked up a little when he saw a clothes horse which was draped with Cindy and Katie's laundered lingerie.

'Boy, you must be the luckiest guy in the world, shacked up with two hot chicks like Katie and Cindy. What did you do, win the lottery?'

'We're just good buddies.' Tony reddened as he flipped the kettle on.

A copy of the Tennessean was laying on the kitchen table. Tex picked it up and took off his shades to get a better look at the picture on the front cover of himself and Katie.

'You sure about that?' he pressed Tony. 'Only I'd hate to butt in on anything. But that Katie, she's something else, ain't she?'

'She's a goddess!' Tony sighed. 'But nope, there's nothing between me and Katie.'

'Cindy?' Tex enquired.

'Nope. Just good friends.'

'You must have a will of iron,' Tex

commented as he watched Tony slide the pizza out of the oven. 'I was thinking about Katie on the way over and what a guy would give to have a girl like that. Do you think that would make a good song? You know, a list of the things you'd actually give — the most precious things you have!'

Tony weighed it up.

'That sounds like a great song.'

They carried the pizza and coffee into the living room and set them on the coffee table next to some yellow legal pads and pens that Tony had put out earlier in preparation.

'You start, then,' Tony said. 'What would you give to have a girl like Katie in your life?'

Tex let out a slow chuckle.

'Well, there's that old Harley out there. You can have that for starters!'

'I'd give you my old Harley . . . ' Tony tested the line with a melody. 'That's a good start.'

He hummed the melody a couple more times, then wrote the line down.

'Your turn,' Tex said. 'What's the most precious thing you own?'

Tony thought hard.

'Picture of my mother?'

'Now we're getting somewhere,' said Tex. 'But let's dig a little deeper here. This ain't just any girl we're talking about, remember, we're talking about Katie Carnegie.'

'You really like her, don't you?'

'Man, are you kidding me? I have never seen a girl who looked so hot.'

'Is it just about looks?' Tony challenged him.

Tex gave him a narrow-eyed sideways look.

'Well, I've only just met her . . . ' he said cautiously. 'Are you saying she's not as nice as she looks?'

'I'm saying she is just as nice as she looks. She's a good friend of mine and I wouldn't like to see her hurt because you thought it was a bit of fun.'

Tony felt his cheeks burning and realised his heart was racing. He was surprised at himself for speaking like that to a big tough guy like Tex. He normally went far out of his way to avoid confrontation. But then, he was also surprised at himself for feeling so strongly. He realised Cindy and Katie had become his family, and he didn't want someone riding into town and upsetting either of them.

To his relief, Tex seemed to get the strength of his message. For a moment, the big guy in the black leather looked put out. Then he cracked an appeasing grin.

'Okay, okay, you can put the shotgun down, big brother! What makes you think I'm so superficial, anyway?'

Tony grinned back.

'Well, if you're really serious about Katie, prove it. What would you really give to have her?'

Tex thought deeply.

'How about . . . the memory of my mother? Is that good enough for ya?'

'Whew!' Tony wrote the line down, happily. 'This is gonna be a strong song, that's for sure!'

As the pizza disappeared and the legal pads filled up with jottings, Tex worked off his hangover. Engrossed in shared creativity, Tony's wariness of the singer evaporated. By the time they were hammering out the melody, guitars cradled in their laps, they were singing lines across the coffee table to each other like life-long buddies.

They just about had the song nailed when Cindy came home, raincoat over her waitress uniform. She'd hoped Tex would be gone by the time she got back — or that he'd ask Katie out on a date or something. She wasn't sure what to make of the guy, and after a rather dejected afternoon thinking about Hank and why they'd split up, she wasn't in the mood for anyone's company except maybe Tony's.

Cindy had never had anything but platonic feelings towards Tony and nor, so far as she knew, had he ever harboured anything but platonic feelings towards her. But there were times when she almost thought a purely platonic marriage to Tony would be pretty darn close to blissful. At least he'd feed her and, unlike every other guy she'd ever met, he'd be the (marginally more) tidy, houseproud one in the relationship.

In short, she decided, Tony would make someone a great wife one day!

As soon as she turned her key in the door and heard the singing carrying through from the living room, however, the black clouds over her head began to clear. Music had always been the biggest thing in her life, and the music Tony and Tex were making right now was the most melodic and soulful she'd heard in a long time.

The moment she heard Tex's rich baritone singing lead to Tony's light tenor harmony, she forgot any reservations about the kind of guy Tex was. Anyone who sang with that much feeling couldn't be all bad.

'Wow, that sounds good!' she enthused, as she burst excitedly into the living room.

Tex smiled up at her from the couch. If, last night, he'd looked like the devil in motorcycle boots, right now he looked rather angelic. Cindy felt a little pang of envy for Katie, who seemed to have made such a big impression on Tex.

'Maybe you can help us out here,' Tex drawled. 'We were just wondering if we could turn this thing around so it's a girl singing about a guy. How 'bout you sing a bit for us?'

'You think it might suit Katie, you mean? Sure, let me have a look.'

Cindy dropped her raincoat on the couch and picked up the pad with the lyrics, while Tony strummed his guitar and sang softly to teach her the melody. She cleared her throat and began to sing softly. She was tired from a long day in Lulu's, and a little self-conscious about standing in front of Tex in her ketchup-smeared waitress uniform, but it always felt good to stretch out her voice.

A couple of lines in, she got choked

up on the line about giving the memory of her mother. She stopped and apologised.

'These are strong words! Let me try again.'

She kicked off her high heels and wriggled her toes into the carpet. Taking a deep breath, she focused on the words on the pad and pushed from her mind the fact that Tex was sitting there watching her, as she started over. This time she sang the line with a catch in her throat that only enhanced its poignancy, before putting her lungs into the chorus as if she were on the stage of the Grand Ole Opry itself.

As she sang, she found herself thinking of Hank. Suddenly, cathartic tears that she'd held in for so long burst from her eyes and streamed in muddy rivers of black mascara down cheeks suddenly red and hot.

By the time she reached the final chorus she wasn't singing the words, she was living them. The last line was supposed to be, What I'd give to have a guy like that, but without even realising she was doing it, she sang instead, What I'd give to have you back.

Tony, too, had tears streaming down his chubby pink cheeks, and Tex didn't look far from crying himself. As moved as they both were by the rendition, however, the change of words sent a lightning bolt through the songwriter in each of them.

They exchanged a look like they had just seen magic performed before their eyes.

At length, Tex spoke in an awed tone. 'I think you just co-wrote a hit song with us, Cindy!'

'Come on!' Cindy laughed shakily to cover her embarrassment as she dried her eyes and cheeks with a tissue. 'I didn't co-write anything. I just . . . '

'You just, like, made the song,' Tony shouted.

'Do you think Katie will like it?'

'Uh-uh,' Tony said levelly. 'This one isn't for Katie.'

'He's right there,' Tex drawled.

'What do you mean?' She was confused. 'Katie needs songs . . . '

But Tony and Tex were both shaking their heads.

'Katie's got a song already,' Tony reminded her. 'It's you that needs a hit, Cindy Coin. This is your song.'

4

Tony was late for his shift at Lulu's — in the excitement of finishing the song, he'd completely forgotten the time. His new best buddy Texan Jack offered to give him a lift on the Harley — 'I've got a spare crash hat.'

Cindy stood on the sidewalk as a cloud of blue smoke coughed from the exhaust and the big bike spluttered into life with a raspy chug that shook the street. Mischievously, Jack took off like a demon and Tony screamed like a schoolgirl on a rollercoaster as he hung on for dear life.

'You two big, crazy fools!' Cindy laughed to herself as the tail light whizzed around the corner, with Tony's legs sticking out like a wishbone and his screams still carrying on the air.

Weak from all the unexpected laughing and crying she'd done in the last few minutes, Cindy walked back into the house with a sigh. In the kitchen, she took off her pink gingham waitress uniform and shoved it in the washing machine with some other laundry waiting to be done.

She pulled on jeans and a T-shirt from the clothes horse and, catching sight of her panda eyes in the mirror, washed off her make-up standing at the kitchen sink.

Where had those tears come from? she wondered as she towelled her face. In a way, they were the good kind of tears — the kind that made you feel better for getting them out.

That was the great thing about a good country song, she reflected, the words said things for you that you couldn't always bring yourself to say in real life. For a long time, she hadn't told anyone how she'd been feeling about Hank. She hadn't even shared it with Tony, and he was about the best listener a girl could have.

The words in the song had really

connected to her sense of loss and longing, and it had given her such a sense of relief to say them aloud.

The other great thing about a song, of course, was that she'd been able to express those feelings without having to tell anyone who she was expressing those feelings about. To Tex and Tony, she was just singing a song they'd written that she happened to find moving. She had no idea who they'd been thinking about when they wrote it, and they in turn thankfully had no idea who she was thinking about as she sang it.

But where had that last line come from? Sure, she missed being in love with Hank, but did she really want him back? And, even if she did, could she ever have him back? Everything about him said he had moved on.

She opened the fridge to see what she could graze on. Tony always left plenty of ready-to-snack goodies in there. She found a slice of pie and pulled up a chair at the kitchen table where that morning's Tennessean still lay face up.

She turned it towards her and gazed at the picture of Katie and Tex. Leaning over her plate, she re-read the article, even though she'd read it over breakfast. There was a quote from Troy Tillman saying how he expected Katie to be a huge star, and a couple of paragraphs explaining that Texan Jack had already built up a big following in country music's second biggest city, Austin, Texas.

Cindy sighed wistfully. How she'd longed to see her own picture splashed on a front page like that, above an article tipping her for the top.

She'd built up a good reputation within the music community over the past five years, and she had to admit that Hank had been instrumental in opening a few doors for her. She often got work singing backing vocals on records by top singers. Songwriters used her to sing demo recordings of the songs they pitched to the stars. When she got up to sing a few songs in one of the tiny music bars that littered the city, she always got a warm reception.

But was that as far as she was destined to go? Everyone told her to keep going. But was the truth that she'd missed her chance? As she gazed at Katie, looking so young, she wondered if she herself had got just that little too old to be the next big star.

She thought back to how excited Tex and Tony had been about this new song, how insistent they were that it was her song, the one that would get her a record deal. She felt a small, familiar tingle of excitement rekindling in her stomach, because she knew it was a great song, and she had connected to it so perfectly that it did indeed feel like her song.

But, after having so many dreams smashed over the past five years, she barely dared to get her hopes up.

⋆ ⋆ ⋆

It was at that moment that Cindy heard an unmistakable raspy chugging sound outside. What on earth was Tex coming back for?

As he killed the engine with metallic splutter, she had one of those self-conscious moments that she used to get with Hank. She'd scrubbed off every scrap of make-up and had pulled on the first jeans and T-shirt that came to hand. Looking down, she now realised the jeans were so faded they might as well have been bleached, and her top was just about fit to wipe a floor with.

Tex rapped loudly on the front door and she leaped up from the table. As she passed the living room door, she saw an unfamiliar guitar propped against the couch and breathed a sigh of relief. So that's what he'd come back for.

'Coming!' she shouted, jamming the guitar into its case and snapping on the catches. Opening the door, she thrust the case into Tex's startled arms just as he put his leg forward to step over the threshold.

Pausing to catch his breath, he gave

her a slow smile.

'Well, thanks for not actually slamming the door in my face.'

Cindy blushed.

'I'm sorry. That was what you came back for, wasn't it?'

'I came back,' Tex grinned, 'because you can't write a hit song and not celebrate. Grab your boots, Cindy, we're going out on the town.'

'Me? I can't go out looking like this?'

'You look perfect to me. You'll need a jacket, though — no bare arms on a motorcycle when the sun's gone down.'

Cindy suddenly knew just the right jacket to wear.

'Just gimme a minute,' she told him, and took the stairs two at a time.

Her over-stuffed wardrobe stood open as always, and she pulled out a soft black leather jacket with fringed sleeves. Before she pulled it on, she ditched the floor-cloth T-shirt and pulled a crisp plain white one over her head. She pushed her feet into the best of several pairs of cowboy boots that littered the floor along with the rest of her shoe collection.

When you don't feel so good, buy shoes. That was her motto. Since she'd split with Hank she'd bought a lot. Then again, Tony would have reminded her, her other motto was: When you feel really good, buy shoes. She'd bought a lot while she'd been with Hank, too.

Realising how quickly she'd become so excited, she briefly asked herself why she was dropping everything to rush off with Texan Jack, and why she was acting like she was going on a date.

But why shouldn't she? It was a long time since she'd been on a date, and while she knew it wasn't really that, it was still Texan Jack Dallas on her doorstep. Who wouldn't get a little excited?

Not wanting to keep him waiting, she snatched a look at herself in the mirror. No make-up, but what the heck? Her rushing about had brought a glow to her face. Her eyes were bright and alive. Without make-up she looked younger and fresher than she remembered.

'Nice look,' said Tex, as she clattered down the stairs in her cowboy boots. Outside, he eased a visor-less helmet over her head and fastened the strap beneath her chin for her. She enjoyed the intimate feel of his fingers brushing her skin as he fiddled with the buckle, and the chance to look closely at his handsome face while it was so close to hers, but his eyes were lowered, focused on what he was doing.

She was still gazing at him when his steely blue eyes flicked back up and met hers. He gave her a grin, then he picked her up by the waist, swung her through the air as if she weighed nothing, and sat her astride the pillion seat of the Harley.

Straddling the shiny white gas tank he kicked the bike into chugging, spluttering life, and the throbbing vibration of the leather pillion seat went right through her, vibrating her bones.

'Hold tight!' Tex grinned over his shoulder.

Cindy hugged herself to the broad, shiny back of his jacket and smelled the leather as she wrapped her arms around his middle. Remembering how he'd deliberately terrified Tony earlier, she began to speak.

'Don't go too fa . . . ' But the Harley was hurtling away from the kerb.

* * *

Hank's black Chevrolet was just turning into the street as the Harley roared away from the kerb. As the bike sped past them, Katie spun around on the shiny mint green leather passenger seat.

'That was Tex and Cindy!'

'Yeah?' Hank was unconcerned.

'Where are they going?' Katie was almost kneeling up on the seat, straining her eyes through the back window as the bike's tail light flared, as Tex paused at the junction before roaring away again.

'I dunno,' said Hank, 'Off on a date somewhere . . . ?'

'Well, let's get after them!'

Hank gave her a sideways look like she was crazy.

'You can't catch a Harley in a Chevy!' he said with a lazy grin.

'He's not taking her to Texas.' Katie was scornful. 'They'll only be going downtown. We'll easily catch up and spot them. Come on, turn this thing around right now!'

Hank checked her face to see if she was serious, and saw that she was. She really was crazy. But what the heck? He didn't mind a bit of craziness, and saying no to pretty girls was something he'd never been good at.

He swung the car towards the kerb then tugged the big, ribbed, shiny white steering wheel the other way. The gleaming black two-ton body leaned heavily over its white-wall tyres, but the big square boat of a car turned surprisingly tightly for such a hefty piece of machinery, and the 50-year-old engine gave quite a kick when Hank straightened the wheel and squeezed the accelerator pedal into the carpet. As the mint-green seat seemed to scoop her up and shove her down the road with a noisy burble from the engine, Katie grinned at Hank and saw that he was grinning too, as they raced off in hot pursuit.

They cruised through the thick Saturday night traffic of Upper Broadway. Suddenly Katie pointed.

'There they are!'

The distinctive white tail of Tex's Harley was parked between two pick-up trucks. The sidewalk was teaming with tourists, but as the Chevy rolled by Hank saw Tex and Cindy cutting through the cowboy-hat-wearing hordes to enter the Silver Dollar Saloon. Tex's arm was around her slim shoulders and their faces were close, laughing after the exhilaration of the motorcycle ride.

Hank felt a strange twinge, but covered it with a grin.

'So whaddya wanna do, gate-crash their date?'

Katie grinned back at him and

answered with relish.

'Yeah I do!'

He shook his head with a chuckle. He liked this girl. He found a parking space on the next block, locked the car and they began to walk back.

A five-piece band was playing good-time country music, out-of-towners were line-dancing in front of the stage and the place was buzzing. Although the saloon was dark, quite a few heads turned as Tex and Cindy walked in. She couldn't tell whether it was because they recognised him from the picture in the Tennessean, or whether it was just because he looked so drop-dead striking. Either way, it was a good feeling to be the girl on his arm. It reminded her of how she used to feel, walking into places with Hank. He had always turned heads. Even when he'd barely known a soul in the business, he had always entered any room looking like he owned the whole darn town.

They found a tall table by the window and hauled themselves up onto high stools where they could soak up the hot dark atmosphere but be far enough from the band and the constant ker-chink-a-chink of the mirror-backed bar that they'd be able to talk.

They had just clinked their glasses together when Hank's white Stetson loomed through the door. Katie homed in behind him like a missile and draped a proprietorial arm around Tex's leather-clad shoulders.

'Well, ain't this quite a surprise?' she gushed. 'Fancy us just bumping into you two!'

Tex took advantage of her closeness to slip an arm around her tiny waist and pull her closer so that he could plant a long kiss on her coquettishly turned, peach-coloured cheek.

'Well, I'm sure glad you're here, Katie,' Tex drawled. 'You're just in time to help us celebrate.'

Cindy smiled ruefully. Being Tex's hot date for the night had been nice while it lasted. All of ten minutes, wasn't it? She watched Tex and Katie canoodling with wistful fondness, but knew she wasn't too put out. It was actually quite a relief that Katie and Hank had showed up. She knew this hadn't really been a date, but she'd started to wonder what she would do if it turned into a date and Tex started to get amorous later!

Now, with Katie and Hank here, it felt good to be out in a social situation, squeezed around a small table with her friends. It was like they were two couples. Katie and Tex, Cindy and Hank. Yep, that felt real comfortable.

'So, what are we celebrating?' Hank asked.

'Cindy, Tony and I just wrote the biggest hit of the year!' Tex held his hands wide apart as if describing the length of some monstrous fish he'd just landed.

Hank raised his eyebrows at Cindy, who just smiled innocently.

'I'm glad someone's written me a hit,' Katie enthused. 'Those songs Troy's been playing me all day have been terrible.'

Tex looked uncomfortable. He took a moment to moisten his lips before making the confession.

'Well, actually, baby doll, this ain't a song for you. It's a song for Cindy.'

'Cindy?' Katie repeated it so loudly heads turned towards their table. Narrowing her eyes she shot Cindy a black look.

Cindy shrugged in silent appeal.

Tex, meanwhile, was leaning excitedly across the table towards to Hank.

'Man, you have gotta hear Cindy sing this song. It's the song that's gonna get her a record contract, and while you've got Troy's ear, you're the man to pull off the deal!'

Now he had Hank's full attention, he went on.

'I like this joint promotion thing you're building with me and Katie, and now here's a third angle. Cindy co-wrote this song with me, I'm gonna have a record coming out, and the other co-writer is Tony, who wrote Katie's song, and it looks like that's gonna be a hit record. So it's like the three of us are all linked. Cindy, Katie and Tony even share a house together. The press and the DJs are gonna love this story!'

Hank smiled and nodded.

'Well, if you get a demo of this song down, Cindy, Tony can do the music and I'll fix up a meeting with Troy. What's this wonderful song all about?'

'Oh, man!' Tex said. 'I've got tears in my eyes just thinking about it. It's about this girl who wants this guy back so bad, she's talking about all the things she'd give to make that happen. When Cindy sang it she just tore us to pieces.'

He shot her an awed look.

'Who were you singing that thing about, anyway?'

Hank and Katie turned to her, expectantly.

With her knees squeezed up against Hank's under the table, she suddenly felt as if her face were on fire. Flustered, she tried to sound breezy as she responded.

'Oh, you know, just . . . guys.'

Desperate to shift the focus of attention, she went on quickly.

'You and Tony wrote most of it before I came home. Who were you writing about?'

Like a tennis audience, Hank and Katie's faces now turned to quiz Tex. Cindy noted that he was a cooler customer than she was. A born stage performer, he revelled in keeping them in suspense for a moment.

'Oh, you know, just . . . girls.'

'Any girls in particular?' Katie teased him.

Tex pretended to consider the question.

'Nope. Although, Tony did spend an awful lot of time talking 'bout you, baby doll.'

'Tony did?' Her jaw fell open.

'He's a dark horse.' Tex smiled. 'But I think he's got the hots for you. He practically pulled a shotgun on me and warned me off.'

'Hang on, this is Tony we're talking

about?' Katie and Cindy exchanged a bemused look.

At that moment, a middle-aged lady with a mid-west accent appeared shyly at Tex's shoulder, a folded copy of the Tennessean in her hand.

'Pardon me, but is this picture of you two? Would you mind if I asked for your autographs?'

Once they'd been recognised, two or three other people came over for autographs, one by one.

Cindy watched the way Tex handled the attention like a true star. He was unfailingly polite, calling everyone 'Ma'am' or 'Sir' or, in the case of one pretty young girl, 'Baby doll.' At the same time, he seemed to slip effortlessly into a slightly larger than life, stage version of himself. His voice became even deeper and sexier than usual, and he almost glowed with that devilish, slightly scary charisma she'd observed in Lulu's the night before.

Katie handled the attention more excitedly and gushingly, but looked as though she could easily come to love it.

Watching proudly but wistfully from the sidelines, Cindy wondered what it would be like to be on the end of an autograph request herself.

* * *

Her parents had been musicians. Neither were famous. Her dad was a bass player and her mom a backing singer, and they worked the road in someone else's band.

When Cindy was about five, they took her to a Dolly Parton concert. Dolly's sparkling dresses and towering blonde wig were just about the most glamorous things she'd ever seen. Afterwards, her mom and dad took her to the stage door, along with hundreds of other folk.

Standing beside her tour bus, its engine rumbling away on permanent idle in the background, Dolly must have signed her name for an hour, while Cindy and her folks waited in line. Not once had she shown any sign if fatigue, boredom or just plain irritation. Cindy had been sitting on her dad's shoulders, and when they reached the front of the queue she towered over the diminutive superstar.

Dolly had beamed up at her and had blown her a kiss.

It wasn't long after that that Cindy's parents were killed in a tour bus wreck on a snowy highway in Nebraska. Cindy was brought up by her grandparents, who though kind didn't really approve of her ambition to be a country star — especially after what had happened to her mom and dad.

As she grew up on the farm with her grandparents, however, Cindy spent every day of her childhood singing Dolly Parton songs, and dreaming of one day being in the position Tex and Katie were now, bestowing signatures on scraps of paper for adoring fans. Looking back, Cindy guessed part of her in country music had likely been a way of feeling close to her departed parents.

But a big part had simply been wanting to be like Dolly, who was the most glamorous woman she'd ever seen. She knew that if she became a star like Dolly her parents would be proud of her.

When she'd stepped off the train five years ago, she'd felt certain she'd have a record deal in a year or two, After all, she had spent her entire life preparing for it.

Yet somewhere during the past few years she'd begun to wonder if it would ever happen, and these days she barely dared to hope. Now, as she watched Katie and Tex living the dream so close to her, that tingle of excitement was back in her stomach. Tex had sounded so impressed when he talked about the song to Hank, and Hank had got that old twinkle back in his own grey-green eyes.

When he'd had his fill of adulation, Tex stretched.

'Why don't we go on to this cool little

place I found last night? It'll be more private there.'

Hank declined with a firm tilt of his head. He frowned at the young man.

'Last night was quite enough for me, Tex.'

'I'll pass, too,' Cindy said. 'It's been a long day.'

Tex grinned.

'Looks like it's just you and me, Katie.'

'Suits me!' She grinned back.

After they'd said their goodbyes, Cindy watched Tex and Katie head for the door, their arms clasped tightly around each other's waists — a perfect picture of young love.

'I hope she knows what she's getting herself into.' Hank was smiling but there was a warning note in his voice.

'What do you mean?' She paused while taking a sip from her glass.

'Word's been filtering up from Texas. Seems Tex has got a bit of a reputation for having a different girl in every city.'

'Do you think we should warn her?'

Hank shrugged.

'Do you think she'd thank us?'

Cindy knew he was right, but still felt a bit guilty.

After a while, she gave a teasing smile.

'To think I could have been Miss Nashville!'

Hank gave her a curious look, but she was happy to let him ponder the mystery. They still had their drinks to finish, and as the band began to play that dreamy old Eagles song about lying eyes, Cindy settled into just enjoying sitting at a tall table with Hank in the Silver Dollar Saloon.

Eventually, after both their glasses had sat empty for a while, Hank stood up and smiled.

'Drive you home?'

Cindy's eyes smiled her thanks.

Walking up Broadway with Hank felt just like old times. It was all Cindy could do not to take his hand. She doubted he would have minded. After all, friends held hands, didn't they?

As she opened the big, fat door of the Chevy, with its familiar little creak, and slid into the shiny, permanent, rump-shaped dent in the bench seat, it was like sliding back in time. She clunked the door shut, closing out the babbling conversations of the sidewalk and the intermingled sounds of several competing country songs drifting out of the various bars, and took a moment to breathe in the familiar smell of the car's big, airy interior. It was an unmistakable mixture of old leather, old suits and Hank's woody cologne.

For a moment, it was like the past five years had never happened. Tilting the creaky old sun-visor to block the glare of a street lamp, she found herself checking her eyes in the vanity mirror to see if they still looked as young and fresh as they had. Maybe, she guessed, though perhaps a little wiser, toughened up by experience and disappointment. She was pleased to see they hadn't lost their hope, though — they hadn't become disillusioned, like the eyes of some of the one-time hopefuls who had waited tables a year or two too many.

Hank turned the key with that old-fashioned scratchy metallic sound and the car gave a little shudder Cindy remembered so well before the engine settled down to its familiar burble beneath the hood. He clicked up the outsize gear shift that stuck out of the steering column, and the car lurched forward against the brake before he let the car roll out, slow and stately, into the traffic.

The radio was always on, low, in Hank's car, tuned to a country station. Suddenly, as the bright lights of Broadway flew by, they were listening to Katie singing I Want Your Body, Cowboy.

'They're playing her song!' Cindy turned up the fat chrome volume knob, which was in the shape of a horse's head. Hank grinned but said nothing until the song was over, quietly savouring the sound of the single coming out, thinly, through the car's half-century old speakers.

When the DJ had finished telling the world a bit about Nashville's newest recording star, Hank turned the volume back down.

'If Tex is right, that could soon be you they're playin'.'

Cindy wished he hadn't said it. If there was one part of her she didn't want to revisit it was all those promises Hank had filled her head with.

They drove on in companionable silence, apart from the soft caress of country music drifting out of the radio, and Hank slid the Chevy into the kerb outside her house. He killed the engine and turned around a little on the roomy bench seat, one elbow resting on the fat, curved top of the seat back.

'Well, I'm intrigued by this new song of yours,' he drawled. 'Are you gonna invite me in and sing it for me?'

In the half light and shadows cast by the sparse street lamps, she eyed him, in his sharp vintage suit, with his carefully oiled retro-hairstyle, parted as if with a ruler and smoothed slickly over his head. On the outside, he hadn't changed a bit. She wondered if he'd changed at all on the inside.

She knew she had.

Over his shoulder, through the driver's window, was the door to her house. She remembered all the times they'd walked over that threshold together, his hand laying lightly but warmly on her shoulder, or on her hip. The physical attraction she felt towards him hadn't changed, but whether he still felt the same pull towards her she couldn't tell. His twinkly grey-green eyes and permanent hint of a smile were hard to read at the best of times.

They had been alone together plenty of times since they'd split, and neither had showed any sign that they hadn't got this friends thing completely under control.

As she remembered the words of the song, though, and the way it had made her well up earlier, the thought of standing in her living room and singing it to Hank made her cheeks burn with embarrassment. She hoped he couldn't see her flushing up in the shadows of the car, and also hoped she didn't sound too flustered as she replied.

'To tell you the truth, Hank, I'm a little bushed. You'll have to hear it when we cut the demo.'

She pulled the lever and opened the door with a creak, letting in some cool night air. Hank didn't look disappointed. He just gave her that inscrutable little wink, same as ever.

As she opened her front door, Cindy turned and watched the big black Chevy slide away. With a heavy sigh, she wondered how long she'd go on standing there, watching those red tail-lights and feeling those same irrational pangs in her middle.

She couldn't go back to him, though, could she? That would just be putting herself through the same old pain all over again.

5

Katie came downstairs in bare feet and pyjamas just as Tony was carving the Sunday roast. Her eyes were as closed as a newborn kitten's, her cascading blonde curls hung in soft tangles on her slim shoulders and the smile on her lips said she was still asleep and dreaming.

'Has Tex phoned?' she asked as she blindly felt her way to a chair at the kitchen table.

'Uh-uh,' Tony murmured.

'Well, it looks like somebody had a good night!' Cindy put aside the Sunday papers to make room for the plates of succulent turkey that Tony was putting on the check tablecloth in front of them. Cindy had thought Katie's pyjamas were white with black polka dots, but on closer inspection the dots proved to be little black hearts.

'What time did you get in this morning?'

'I think I'm in love.' Katie sighed dreamily as she felt for her plate and cutlery, her eyes still closed.

Then her pretty brow creased.

'And Tex has just left town for ten days of shows in Alabama. How unfair is that?'

Cindy and Tony exchanged a look as Tony spooned out steaming vegetables. She remembered what Hank had said about Tex having a girl in every town. She felt guilty for not having warned Katie, but now was hardly the moment to mention it.

'Well, you better get used to him going away,' Tony said gently. 'Because that's what you get when you fall for a guy whose home address is a tour bus!'

'Tony speaks from experience,' Cindy joked.

Katie half opened one eye and gave Cindy a surprisingly hard look between her lush blonde lashes.

'So, Cindy, what exactly were you

doing sneaking off on a date with my man last night?'

'Like I said before, I saw him first!' Cindy teased. 'That wasn't a date, silly. I didn't even have any make-up on! Besides, Tony and I are happily married, aren't we, Tony?'

'The happiest.' Tony said gravely as he took his place at the head of the table. 'Now, if we can just take a moment to say thanks for what we are about to receive?'

'Thanks, Tony!' Cindy and Katie cried simultaneously, and they all tucked in hungrily.

Some hours later, still in her pyjamas, Katie was sitting cross-legged on the couch, hugging a cushion to her belly. She mostly kept her eyes closed, still recovering from a night on the town with Tex, but occasionally opened one eye to gaze accusingly at the phone, which still hadn't rung.

All around her, Tony built a recording studio in their living room — a professional-quality microphone on a chrome stand, electric guitar and electric bass, a digital piano keyboard. It was all connected through a tangle of wires to a laptop computer on the coffee table.

Every instrument, and its discarded case, all which littered what was left of the floor space, was chipped and worn from having travelled further and wider than most people would travel in a lifetime. Some of the equipment was Tony's, the rest he had gathered together in an after-lunch whip-round among his neighbours.

In East Nashville, amplifiers and bass guitars were swapped and loaned the way guys in other neighbourhoods swapped and borrowed lawnmowers and electric drills!

For the price of a few beers and some homemade pancakes, he could have assembled a band. But Tony was proficient on most instruments, and went from one to another, playing and recording, building up a musical arrangement layer by layer.

Cindy, however, was having doubts about recording What I'd Give. After a couple of half-hearted rehearsals, when she just couldn't get a tight dryness out of her voice, she sat down with the legal pad containing the lyrics propped on her knees.

'You know, maybe Katie should sing this, after all.'

'Yeah,' Katie agreed. 'I could do a great version of that song, just thinking 'bout Tex. What I wouldn't give to have that guy back here with me right now!'

She hugged the cushion tighter and wriggled seductively on the couch.

'Why don't you just call him?' asked Cindy, as Katie's eyes flicked towards the silent phone for the gazillionth time.

'No way!' Katie protested. 'The girl should never ever be the first to call the guy!'

'That's why this is such a great song,' Tony explained as he tapped a key on the keyboard and checked the recording level on the laptop. 'It says the things you girls are too proud to come out and say to a guy in real life.'

'So you guys wouldn't be too proud to say it?' Katie challenged him, her voice sarcastic.

'Sure, we're exactly the same.' Tony grinned. 'But if love ran smooth, who'd need country songs?'

Cindy was still wringing her hands about recording the song. Her dilemma was made worse by the fact she could hardly tell them that the reason she was reluctant to make the demo was because Hank would hear it, and she was scared he'd guess she was singing about him.

'Why don't we let Katie just give it a try?' she suggested again.

Tony's kindly voice took on a firm tone he seldom used, but which always got Cindy's attention.

'I've already written a song for Katie, and Katie's already got a record deal. You need a deal, Cindy, and this is the song that's gonna make it happen for you.'

'Tony's right,' Katie admitted generously. 'Just think what it will be like. You, me and Tex, all bringing records out at the same time!'

Cindy's stomach was in a knot. Of course a record deal was what she'd always wanted. And yet . . .

'How 'bout I try one of your other songs? Maybe I'm In The Mood For A Cheatin' Song?'

Tony rolled his eyes.

'Anybody could sing that song. But when you sang What I'd Give last night . . . Cindy, nobody has ever connected to a song the way you did! Tex and I had tears in our eyes. If we can get that performance on disc it'll be the hit of the year.'

Katie studied Cindy through narrowed eyes, curious.

'What's your problem with this song, anyway?'

Cindy felt cornered. Clutching the legal pad defensively across her middle, she tried to laugh, but her throat was so dry nothing came out.

'Oh, I don't know. It's just . . . ' She flapped her hand, flustered. 'I dunno,' she finished lamely.

Tony stood up with a sigh.

'I'll fix some more coffee. Anybody want pancakes while I'm at it?'

'I do!' Katie and Cindy said simultaneously. With Katie missing a man who hadn't phoned, and Cindy missing a man she couldn't bring herself to name, comfort food was definitely in order!

When Tony was out of the room, Katie probed further.

'So, who is he? The guy you wish you had back.'

Cindy gazed at her and couldn't believe the pressure building up inside of her — the need she felt to unburden herself. Normally, the one person she would have confided in was Tony.

But sometimes you could be too close to someone, and in this instance Tony was that someone. He had been there for her so much when she'd ended it with Hank. He'd literally held her in his arms while she soaked his shirt through with her tears. He'd held her hand through the painful process of getting back to just good friends terms with Hank.

If Tony thought she was thinking of getting back together with Hank romantically, well, it wasn't that he'd be unsympathetic — Tony didn't have an unsympathetic bone in his body — but perhaps he'd have opinions. Without meaning to, he might say something that would push her in one direction or the other and, being that it was Tony, she'd listen to him. But, on this occasion, could she trust him to be right? She wanted to tell Katie, but could she trust her not to mention it to Tony?

At length, she just smiled, playing for time while she searched for words.

'Just this guy, you know?'

Katie nodded and looked again at the phone that wouldn't ring.

'Guys, eh?'

Cindy felt a little better just for sharing that much.

When Tony came back with the coffee and pancakes and they all tucked in, Katie tackled him in jest.

'So, come on, who did you write this song about?'

Embarrassed at being put on the spot, Tony used the excuse of a full mouth not to answer for a long time. Having given himself time to come up with an answer, he finally spoke.

'You should never ask who a song's about, because at the end of the day, a song's just a song. It becomes something different in its own right. I mean, Tex, Cindy and I all brought something to this song, so who can say it's really about one person or another?'

'Come on,' Katie pressed him. 'You can do better than that! Who did it start out being about?'

Tony squirmed, evasively,

'Aw, you know . . . '

Then, realising how much Katie was feeling rejected by Tex's failure to call her, he decided to confide a little.

'It was Tex who actually came up

with the idea. Don't ever tell him I told you this, but if you have to know the truth, he said he came up with the idea because he was thinking about you.'

Katie's eyes grew wide.

'He actually said that? You mean all that stuff in the song is how he feels about me?'

'Well maybe not all the stuff,' Tony cautioned. 'Like I said, three people wrote those words.'

'So why doesn't he phone and just tell me all those things?'

Tony exchanged a look with Cindy and said gently,

'He's on a tour bus. Maybe he just can't get a signal.'

'You're saying they never stop at a gas station with a payphone?'

Tony shrugged awkwardly. He didn't have an answer. So he stuffed some pancake in his mouth.

As Cindy bit into her own pancake, however, she began to wonder if the answer was because Tex just couldn't bring himself to say those powerful words to Katie.

Maybe that was why he'd been so keen to turn the song around so that it was a girl singing to a guy. Perhaps he didn't want to sing it himself, in case Katie guessed he was singing about her.

She knew how he felt. Sometimes it was scary to come right out and say what you felt in case the other person didn't feel the same way.

But, she suddenly realised, that was also the beauty of saying it in a song. Because, as Tony said, a song was just a song — nobody really knew who a song was about or if it was just completely made up.

So you got to unburden yourself of what you were feeling without having to admit you said it at all.

She put her plate on the coffee table.

'I think I'm ready to sing this thing. But would you guys do me a favour and wait in the kitchen while I sing it?'

Tony sprang from his chair. As long as they finally got the song recorded, he would have waited anywhere!

Urgently beckoning Katie to get herself off the couch, he fiddled a moment with the laptop.

'You know how to work this, don't you?' he fretted. 'Just click there when you're ready to sing.'

6

If the average 20-something man and woman stood holding hands in the kitchen, gazing excitedly into each other's eyes the way Katie and Tony were, and if they were listening to an achingly romantic country song, then a casual outside observer might have felt pretty certain what was going through their minds.

If the couple then grabbed each other in a bear hug and buried their faces in each other's hair, then the observer might have thought their initial assumption was correct.

But in Katie and Tony's case they would have been wrong.

'That sounded amazing!' they both screamed, simultaneously.

In the living room, Cindy allowed herself a smile at the sound of her friends whooping it up in the kitchen.

Getting that out of her system had been like taking a ton weight off her shoulders. She was just glad they hadn't been in the living room with her, watching the glistening tears streaming down her face as she sang. If she hadn't been alone, pouring everything she had into the song without the distraction of embarrassment, she doubted she would have got through it.

Wiping her soaking cheeks with the back of her hand, she took a deep breath to compose herself, and turned to the window, just in time to see Hank's black 1957 Chevrolet slide up to the kerb. In sudden panic, she picked her way over the instruments and cases that littered the floor and made a break for the stairs.

'Will somebody let Hank in?' she shouted. 'I'm going to the bathroom!'

Tony opened the door.

Hank was in one of his treasured vintage outfits as ever, literally wearing his Sunday best. With the afternoon sun gleaming off his oiled hair he looked as if he were all ready for a country church service in the 1950s.

'Just dropped by to see how y'all getting on with the demo,' he drawled.

'We're just about to play it back!' Tony said, excited. 'Come in, come in.'

Hank did as he was invited, and looked particularly happy to have dropped by when he caught sight of Katie in her pyjamas.

Upstairs in the bathroom, Cindy spun the hot and cold taps and hastily washed the tears from her eyes. As she hurriedly but carefully applied some make-up in the mirror, she heard her song drifting full-blast through the floorboards beneath her feet.

With Tony's expert backing arrangement it sounded like a proper record. As she listened to her own smoky contralto storming into the chorus with a heady mixture of heartbreak and strength, she believed she sounded pretty darn good. The words, meanwhile, tore at her so much she almost had to wash off her make-up and start all over again.

Downstairs, Tony played the song again. As the music filled the house, Cindy ran into her bedroom and wondered what on earth to put on. She was supposed to be relaxing at home on a Sunday, so it couldn't be too showy, but she couldn't let Hank see her like this.

As always, her wardrobe stood open, too full to ever be closed. There were chests of drawers she couldn't close either. Piles of clothes were heaped on chairs, and dresses in hangers hung two deep from the picture rail. The floor was a sea of shoes.

Why did she never have a thing to wear?

Sitting in the armchair beside the fireplace, surrounded by musical instruments and cases, Hank gazed at the laptop and nodded his head slowly as the song came to an end for the third time.

Tony waited expectantly as Hank sat in silence, his eyes still fixed on the laptop. Unable to stand it any longer, Tony spoke.

'So, whaddya think?'

At length, Hank looked up and blinked, as if he'd momentarily been in a trance. He shook his head as if to clear it. Then he showed a large, perfect white grin.

'I think you're right. That's a darn number one hit!'

'Do you think you can get Cindy a deal with it?'

'Well, if that performance won't do it, nothing will. Put it on a CD for me. Troy's in the studio with Katie this week, so I'll use the opportunity to play it for him.'

Tony hesitated.

'This isn't a song for Troy to put on Katie's album, remember.'

'Although I could probably sing it just as well . . . ' Katie put in sulkily.

Tony shot her a sharp look and Katie folded her arms as she said in a chastened tone, 'Just kidding.'

Turning back to Hank, Tony looked earnest.

'Cindy needs a record deal, Hank.

She deserves it, and she co-wrote this song, anyway.'

Hank looked from the songwriter to Katie, and gave a reassuring nod.

'Do you think I wouldn't want to be the manager of two hot singers?'

Cindy, who had been lingering in the hall, finally plucked up the courage to come into the living room.

'Hi, Hank,' she said with what she hoped was casualness. 'What do you think of the song?'

He sat up straight and gave her a look that made her stomach tighten like a clenched fist.

'I think it's a masterpiece,' he said in an awed tone. 'As for the performance? You've never sounded better.'

Suddenly unable to meet his gaze, she muttered, 'Thanks,' and ducked away from his scrutiny to sit on the couch beside Tony.

'Who's coming downtown to celebrate?' Hank enthused.

'I think I'll pass,' Tony said. 'I've got to get all this stuff back later, and I want to work on the mix of the song first.'

'Cindy, you up for it?'

She was tempted — too tempted. The song having stirred her emotions up into such a sandstorm, the thought of going out on the town with Hank was suddenly as scary as it was exciting. She didn't trust herself to be thinking straight, and deep down felt she needed time to let things settle down in case she rushed into anything without thinking and ended up making a big fool of herself.

'Aw.' She flapped her hand, slightly flustered. 'I've got work in the morning. I think I'll stay here with Tony.'

'I'll come!' Katie told him.

As Katie stood up, Cindy looked at her in fleeting horror. She thought of changing her mind and agreeing to come, but she knew it would just make her sound foolish. So she said nothing, and tried not to notice the sudden light in Hank's grey-green eyes as they flicked appreciatively up the length of

Katie's heart-spotted pyjamas.

Most people wouldn't even have detected a change in Hank's inscrutable features. But Cindy knew Hank's little looks well — especially that kind. Besides, Katie was probably the most gorgeous woman in Nashville. It would take a strong man not to have a gleam in his eye.

Feeling Hank's gaze, Katie looked down at her pyjamas and blushed.

'I'll just go and put something on.'

As they listened to her bare feet hurrying up the stairs, Tony said something to Hank about whether he thought the song needed some pedal steel guitar, but Cindy wasn't really listening. She was remembering all those little stabs of jealousy and doubt she'd had all the time she was dating Hank.

His work had meant he was always at parties or in bars or clubs while she was waitressing at Lulu's. He always had the number of half a dozen girl singers. How was she to know what was work and what was pleasure?

Katie was back in less than two minutes. She had put on a short, floaty blue dress that showed off the length of her bare arms and legs. Apart from a few seductively stray corkscrews, her unwashed blonde curls were all pulled up from her neck and hidden beneath an outsize steamboat cap of the sort Twiggy might have worn over in London in the swinging 60s.

Cindy envied her ability to go from pyjamas to catwalk so quickly. Katie hadn't bothered with make-up, of course. But then, at her age, with a face like that, who needed it?

Just wait till you're a bit nearer to 30, Cindy thought wryly. But she knew she was kidding herself. Even when Cindy had been Katie's age she'd taken just as long tied up in anxious knots over what clothes to wear as she did these days.

Girls like Katie had a way of looking effortlessly poised and unselfconscious that Cindy had never ever possessed.

'Ready, Hank?' Katie purred as she

stood in the doorway.

He turned to Cindy.

'Are you sure you won't join us?'

Again she hesitated, torn. But she couldn't go back to all the anxiety Hank had caused her in the past. She looked away.

'No, you two go.'

'Well, all right,' he drawled.

As he bid them good evening and walked to the door, Katie looked at Cindy and Tony with narrowed eyes.

'If Tex calls, tell him I've gone on a date!'

Flopping back on the couch, Cindy wondered if she'd done the right thing. She heard the front door slam, then the twin clunks of the Chevy doors followed by the sound of the engine as the big black car pulled away.

Beside her, Tony clicked the laptop and started playing What I'd Give again. She knew he was only having to listen to the mix to work out where it could be improved, but she wished he'd picked a different moment.

* * *

Later, when Tony was fully satisfied with the recording and had burned a CD for Hank, Cindy sat in the armchair and sipped hot chocolate while she watched him tearing down the equipment, carefully putting instruments in their cases and rolling up leads.

At length, she leaned towards him.

'Did you ever have someone who broke your heart but who you really wished you could have back? You know, like in the song?'

He was kneeling on the carpet, dismantling the microphone stand. Because they knew each other well enough not to need to rush their answers, he took a while to consider the question.

Eventually he sat back on his haunches.

'Well, there was this girl in school . . .'

He sighed, and his face suddenly took on a rosy glow as he gazed upwards, at a memory he seemed to be picturing just above the fireplace.

'She had the most beautiful blonde hair you ever saw. I used to carry her books, pick her flowers, write little love songs and sing them to her. We'd tell each other that we'd always be together. But one day her dad got a new job, and she moved with her family out to California.'

He looked down and drew in his breath with a soft whistle.

'We said we'd write every day, and I did for a while. But I guess she just kinda got on with her life. Today she could be anywhere.'

'What was her name?' Cindy asked gently.

'Maybeline.' He sighed blissfully.

Cindy blinked, and fought hard to keep a straight face as she responded in a level voice.

'Sorry? May . . . ?'

' . . . beline,' Tony murmured.

At that moment, Cindy could see that he wasn't really in the room with her at all. His mind was far away in a distant memory. At length, he spoke.

'Sometimes I wonder if she ever thinks of me. I know I still think about her a whole lot.'

Eventually, he seemed to come back to the present and resumed packing the microphone in its case.

'How old were you?' Cindy enquired, curious.

Tony shrugged.

'First grade.'

7

Katie was recording her album at Nashville's historic Bradley Barn studios, where everyone from Patsy Cline to Elvis had made classic recordings. When they broke for lunch, she took a cab to Lulu's. Sometimes Tony's pancakes were the only comfort food that would do.

'Coming right up!' Tony said as he bustled into the kitchen.

As Katie perched herself on a bar stool, Cindy filled her cup with 'drip' from the always steaming coffee-pot.

'How's the recording going?' Cindy asked.

'Nrrrr,' said Katie.

Standing behind the bar in her pink gingham waitress uniform, Cindy took a good look at the girl. She was wearing skin-tight white designer jeans and a tiny, soft pink leather jacket that would have cost Cindy a month's wages at

Lulu's. I Want Your Body, Cowboy was starting to get played on the radio a lot, and Hank reckoned it would be in the charts next week.

But Katie didn't look like a girl in the process of recording a debut album for which stores across America had already placed advanced orders of a million copies.

She looked like a girl who'd accidentally thrown a winning lottery ticket out with the garbage!

'Tex still not phoned?' Cindy asked, sympathetically.

Katie wrinkled her nose.

'And don't ask me if I've tried to call him. His phone's always either turned off or not working, so I can't even leave him a message!'

She turned to Cindy with a pleading expression in her clear blue eyes.

'It's so frustrating. There are pictures and reviews from his shows all over the internet, but for the sake of a simple phone call he might as well be on the moon!'

'Troy and the record company people

must be in touch with him pretty often,' Cindy ventured.

Katie narrowed her eyes.

'I asked Troy if he's spoken to Tex, but they're all covering for him!' Her tone was venomous.

Cindy was sympathetic. It was Thursday now, so most of the week had passed since Tex left town.

'Maybe he's just busy with the shows . . . ' she said, lamely.

Katie gave her a disparaging look. Then she rested her chin on her fists.

'Naw. I've just got to face it. He's not interested.'

She let out a heavy sigh and poked a finger at the corner of her eye.

'I know you think I'm crazy, and I know it was only one night, but he really made me feel like he loved me. I guess that's how he makes all the girls feel, then he just hops on that bus of his, heads off to another town and meets someone else!'

'You can't know he's like that,' Cindy protested.

But Katie gave her a knowing look, and Cindy had to admit the girl probably had a point.

Cindy remembered her brief moment of giddy excitement when Tex showed up on her doorstep on Saturday night, and she wasn't the most easily impressed of females. She often got asked on dates, and more often than not turned the invitation down. Confused as she was feeling over Hank, she had not been feeling particularly open to romance on Saturday.

Yet one smile from Tex had had her running about like a 16-year-old who'd never been kissed. She could guess how easy Tex would find it to pick up more susceptible women. What was more, she doubted a guy like Tex would possess such a power and not exercise it regularly.

Briefly, she remembered the touch of his fingers as he'd fastened the strap of her motorcycle helmet. She recalled the thrill as he'd lifted her so effortlessly off her feet and swung her high through the air to put her on the back of his crazy Harley Davidson. Not for the first time, she wondered what would have happened if Katie and Hank hadn't showed up in the Silver Dollar that night.

Would she have ended up as Tex's Nashville girl?

She liked to think the answer was no, but the truth was, she would have been tempted. So she could well imagine what Katie must have felt like, hung out to dry on a barstool in Lulu's while Tex smooth-talked some new cutie in Mobile, Alabama.

Cindy knew what it was like to be loved and then left out in the cold. Still, even her sisterly empathy couldn't quite stop her pressing with a little frosty bite in her voice.

'So, have you had any more dates with Hank?'

Katie laughed, and looked relieved to change the subject.

'That wasn't a date,' she said in mock horror. 'Hank's just my manager.'

In her heart, Cindy knew that was true, but she'd wanted the relief of having Katie confirm it.

That Sunday night, laying on her bed fully dressed and thinking, Cindy heard Hank's Chevy pull up outside. He left the engine running and she heard just the one door open and close before the car pulled away again. Smiling to herself, she could almost hear him drawl, 'Tomorrow's a work day. Get an early one.'

He was taking Katie's recording career seriously.

Nevertheless, Katie was a gorgeous girl, Hank was an attractive man and the two were working closely together. There must surely be a degree of attraction, and Cindy had felt a serious pang as she watched them leave the house together. Although it was none of her business what they got up to, when she heard Katie come home tonight she felt the kind of relief a mother feels when she hears a daughter get home safely after a date.

She stood up, got ready for bed and turned out the light feeling strangely contented, knowing everything was still as it was.

* * *

'He spent most of the evening talking about you,' Katie pouted the following day.

'He did?' Cindy wished she didn't sound so interested.

'Yeah, about how he's gonna get you an amazing deal with Troy. How your single's gonna be so big. How he's gonna do this and how he's gonna do that . . . Seems to me like Hank and Tex have both forgotten about me!'

Cindy smiled ruefully. She could well imagine Hank enthusing about all the things he was 'gonna do'. She'd heard it all plenty of times before, ever since she had fallen off the kerb into his arms all those years ago.

'Well, at least he actually got you a deal,' she reminded Katie. 'He still hasn't tied anything up with Troy for me.'

'Order 28!' Tony hollered, as he came bustling out of the kitchen with Katie's pancakes.

At the same time, the bell jangled over the door as a couple of customers came in. Cindy picked up her coffee-pot and went over to their booth to take their order.

After she'd taken the order through to Tony in the kitchen, she rejoined Katie across the bar.

Between mouthfuls, Katie was still mulling over Hank.

'I don't know why you split up with him. I can tell he still likes you, and he's quite a hunk . . . '

Cindy laughed.

'Sounds as if you quite like him yourself, the way you're raving over him!'

Katie wrinkled her nose.

'Hank's a good friend, but he's way too old for me — and he's really not my type at all.'

Cindy smiled wryly, and suddenly

felt about a hundred years old. Hank was only about a year older than she was, and she was only five or six years older than Katie. Conscious of her gingham waitress uniform, and the pink shoes that hurt her feet, while Katie was sitting there so fresh-faced and skinny in her designer clothes, she wondered how old and dowdy she looked in the younger girl's eyes.

'Tex is my kind of man,' Katie said warmly. 'Or, at least, he would be . . . '

She gazed away, wistfully, then went on with conviction.

'We just felt so right together. You ever had that feeling when you just know that he's the one you could spend the rest of your life with?'

Cindy rested her elbows on the bar.

'Oh, yeah, I have had that feelin'.' Her voice had fallen to a soft whisper.

'With Hank?' Katie said softly.

'Mmmm-hmmm.'

'So, what went wrong? He cheat on you or something?'

Cindy slowly drew in her breath.

'Not that I could ever say for sure, although I guess I was always the jealous and suspicious kind. I was insecure, I guess, and that didn't help. Plus, he was always filling my head with these big dreams that never came to anything. He used to drive me crazy.'

Katie nodded sympathetically while she ate her pancake.

'He seems pretty grounded to me. Everything he's said he's gonna do, he's done. Maybe he's grown up a bit.'

'Maybe he has.'

Cindy considered. Hank did seem calmer and more settled these days. Then again, perhaps he'd always been that way and the problem had actually been with her.

Perhaps if you got that insecure around the calmest of guys you'd eventually drive them crazy. But would she be any different if she got back together with him now?

As if reading her thoughts, Katie looked up at her.

'D'you ever think of getting back

together with him and trying again?'

Cindy felt her heart quicken a little at the thought. But maybe with certain people it all went wrong if you got too close, and you really were better off being just good friends.

'But what is it with a guy like Tex?' Katie demanded, although whether she were talking to Cindy or herself or just the air in front of her, Cindy couldn't tell. 'How can a guy make you feel like he loves you with all his heart, then just kiss you goodbye and you never hear another word?'

Cindy put her hand on Katie's arm and passed her a napkin to wipe her suddenly watery eyes. She doubted if womankind would ever come up with an answer to that question.

If they did, it would be the day they stopped writing country songs.

* * *

Cindy and Tony had just got home from Lulu's when the phone began ringing in the living room.

'I'll get it,' Tony said.

As Cindy shrugged off her raincoat and hung it up, her ears pricked up at Tony's words.

'Hi, Tex! How's it going in Alabam'?'

Cindy went and stood in the entrance to the living room, watching Tony talk for a while.

'Yeah, she's right here. I'll just get her. Cindy, it's Tex!'

Startled, Cindy pointed at herself and mouthed, 'He wants to talk to me?'

Tony beckoned her, while nodding.

Raising her eyebrows, Cindy took the phone from him.

'Hi, Tex.'

His distinctive drawl slid into her ear like chocolate sauce poured slow, hot and steaming.

'How ya doin', Cindy doll? Hank got your record deal yet?'

'Not yet,' she admitted, and then couldn't stop herself adding, 'You know Hank.'

'Well, I've got some good news. I'm

coming back to town to record next week, and I've just written an amazing new song I'd love you to sing a duet with me on.'

'Me?' Cindy squeaked. 'I thought you were supposed to be recording duets with Katie.'

'Yeah, yeah, we're gonna do that as well. But Katie's a soprano. Your voice is a little lower and darker. I think it will blend a lot better with mine, especially on this particular song. It really needs that aching, heartbroke thing you do.'

'Well, it's your record.'

But she began to feel a tingle of excitement in her stomach. She'd sung backing vocals on plenty of albums over the years, but who ever noticed the backing vocals?

A duet was a whole different ballgame. She'd never been that prominently featured on a record before. And while, yes, Hank said he was gonna get her a record deal of her own, she'd heard enough of Hank's 'gonnas' to know they didn't always come true. Tex already had a record deal, so if he wanted her to sing a duet with him, it was really going to happen. Next week, by the sound of it!

Feeling herself slip from waitress mode into singer mode, she asked him what the song was called.

Tex seemed to hear the shift of gear in her voice, for his own voice grew warmer and more excited, that of one musician talking with another.

'It's called Missing You Miles. It was building up in me all week after we pulled out of town, and it all came together on the bus after the show last night. It's about this singer, although I might change it to a trucker or a soldier — I'm still working on it.

'The point is, it's about this guy who meets this girl and falls really heavily in love with her. Only, his work takes him out of town all the time. So one verse is sung by him, out on the road, missing her, and the other verse is sung by the girl, who's stuck back in town, thinking about him. Then the two voices come together on the chorus.'

'Sounds great!' Cindy enthused. 'Is it about anyone we know?'

Tex chuckled. It was a very sexy sound to hear so intimately in her ear and she wondered if he thought she was flirting with him, although that hadn't been what she meant.

After they talked a bit more about the song, Cindy felt bold enough to ask him about Katie.

'Have you called her yet?'

Tex paused then spoke awkwardly.

'I've been meaning to. You know what it's like on the road. It's always hard finding the time.'

You found time to call me, Cindy thought, reproachfully. She hesitated to poke into someone else's business, but she couldn't help thinking about how dejected Katie had looked in Lulu's earlier. Slouched over her plate at the bar, she'd been barely able to take an interest in the album she was supposed to be making across town.

She wondered if Katie would thank her for getting involved. She doubted it — Katie had her pride.

If Tex was going to call her, she'd want it to be off his own bat, not because he'd been shamed into it.

But Cindy still didn't like to see Katie feeling so rejected. It connected too closely with her own sense of loss.

At length, she spoke in a dry voice.

'She really likes you, you know.'

Tex didn't answer. There was a long, uncomfortable silence.

'Well, I gotta go, baby doll, they're calling me for the sound check. But I can't wait to get back to town and sing this song with you next week. Tell Tony I want to write some more with him, too.'

'Will do,' she answered, sadly.

She'd just put the phone down when she heard the front door open and slam again. Katie came into the room, looking hopeful.

'Has Tex called?'

Cindy exchanged a look with Tony.

'Tony, did you say we were having that special chicken pie of yours?'

* * *

A late evening session had been booked at the Bradley Barn. Troy recorded the backing tracks with the band during the day, but Tex wasn't a daytime kind of a guy. He liked to record at an hour that approximated with his performances on stage, once he'd fully woken up and got his voice warmed up.

Cindy and Tex were alone in the vocal booth, with a glass front and soft green sound-absorbent padding on the other three walls. Beyond the glass, the piano and guitars that littered the main studio stood unattended in muted lighting. The only other people around were Troy and a sound engineer, behind another glass partition in the control room on the far side of the studio.

It was an intimate setting, facing Tex a few feet away across their twin microphones, made even more intimate as Tex had dimmed the lights in the vocal booth to a soft glow, to enhance the romantic mood of the song.

It wasn't usual to dress up for recording sessions — what you sounded like was more important than what you looked like. But, being as it was Tex, Cindy had made an effort with her clothes. After much deliberating, she'd picked her best, tight black jeans, her shiniest black cowboy boots with a dinky stiletto heel and a well-cut white T-shirt.

Tex was wearing black leather trousers, a heavily studded belt and a black T-shirt, with his raven hair slicked back like a young Elvis.

Cindy could see exactly why Katie had fallen so heavily for him. As she sang her verse and gazed into Tex's face across the microphones, she thought about Katie, moping about all week, waiting for a phone call that never came.

She felt Katie's pain, deep inside her,

and poured it into the words on Katie's behalf.

When it was her turn to stand silent and watch Tex singing his words of longing directly into her eyes, she thought about Hank and all the love they'd shared. As she realised how much she missed the feel of his arms around her, she felt the beginnings of tears prickling in her eyes.

She and Tex brought their voices together on the achingly lonesome chorus, each expressing how they really felt about someone they were missing a whole lot. All of a sudden Cindy knew a bit of magic was being recorded here.

She saw it in Tex's slightly glistening eyes, too. As the final notes of the song faded in her earphones, he smiled wistfully and blew her a kiss across the microphones.

Troy's voice, on the intercom, cut through the vocal booth like a railway station announcement.

'That was beautiful, so beautiful! I'm so glad Hank persuaded me to give you a record deal, Cindy. I don't know why I didn't listen to him all these years he's been bugging me. Take five, you guys, while I listen back to what we've got and see if we need to overdub anything.'

There was a small recreation room just down the corridor from the studio, with a pool table, sofas, a water-cooler, a glass-fronted fridge full of cans and a filter coffee-pot on permanent brew. With no-one else in the room as they came in, Tex idly rolled a pool ball across the green baize with his hand. Cindy went to the coffee-pot out of force of habit.

'Drip, Tex?'

Tex chuckled.

'Don't you ever take off that waitress uniform?'

Cindy looked down at her smart jeans and T-shirt and realised with a smile that, yep, in her mind she was still wearing ketchup-smeared pink gingham. She poured them a couple of cups, and sat down across from Tex on the corner couch.

'Don't you ever stop writing songs about things you ought to be saying in real life?' she challenged him, goodnaturedly, but pointedly nonetheless.

He feigned puzzlement.

'Come on.' She gave him a playful little tap on the leg with the pointed toe of her cowboy boot. 'You weren't singing that song to me back there.'

Tex put a hand over his heart, sagged on the couch and pretended she'd stabbed him.

'Aw, baby doll, you're tearing me up when you say things like that.'

Cindy smiled warmly. It was kinda fun, flirting around with Tex. But she wasn't about to let him charm his way off the hook.

'And what about What I'd Give? Tony told me you were thinking about Katie when you wrote that.'

Tex looked nervous.

'He didn't tell Katie, did he?'

''Course he didn't,' she lied. 'But I just don't get it with you two. Since you've been back in town you've been all over her like a rash, but when you were out in Alabama you didn't give her a single call.'

Tex looked smug, and Cindy knew why. When Tex got back to Nashville, Katie had tried to give him the arctic treatment, but Tex had managed to melt her cold front with just a couple of mock-hurt smiles and a few sexily drawled 'baby dolls'.

Since then, they'd been inseparable every moment Tex wasn't in the studio. If Hank hadn't taken her out tonight to stop her distracting Tex from his work, she would have been hanging around waiting for him right now.

Knowing Tex would be off on the road again in a couple of days, Cindy wished Katie had put up a bit more resistance to his charms — just as she felt briefly moved to slap that smug smile off his face right now!

Still, Tex had clearly been living on charm since he first smiled up out of a baby stroller to woo his mother's friends as she pushed him around the block, back in Houston twenty-four years ago. He was a hard guy to dislike, and Cindy couldn't help feeling it wasn't all charm. There was something warm and genuine about him behind that swaggering, tough guy image.

She had to admit, too, that he and Katie looked wonderful together. If ever she'd seen a picture of two beautiful people in love, it was right there in the looks buzzing back and forth between their eyes as Katie sat on Tex's lap, clowning around with him, their noses barely apart.

So why hadn't he called Katie from the road? And would it be any different next time?

At length, Tex responded with a sigh to the question hanging in the air.

'Have you ever been out on the road, Cindy?'

She shook her head, intrigued.

'I've been out there since I was 16,' he drawled. 'Me and my buddies with all our amps and guitars piled into a beat-up station wagon, following the honky tonk trail out of Houston to Austin and San Antone. Then we got a van and started playing bigger places and going further a-field. Finally we got the bus and started living a little more comfortably on the road. But still it's the same life — a different city every night, out on the endless highway for weeks and months at a time.'

He gave her a little grin which nevertheless held very little happiness.

'Sometimes my mom barely recognises me! But the thing is, sometimes you meet a girl you really like, and you find you only see her a couple of days every month or so — less, if the place you met her is out in Laredo or somewhere. Yeah, you can phone and there's email, and sometimes they say they'll wait for you.

'But a lot of times they don't. And why should they live that lonely kind of life, when they can marry some guy who works down town and comes home every night at six?'

He let out another sigh and shook his head, sadly.

'Sometimes it's better not to get too close to anyone. It's better for you and its better for them.'

Poor Katie, Cindy thought. And poor Tex.

Troy's train-announcer voice crackled out of the rec room intercom.

'Wakey-wakey, you guys! We've got a slight foot-tap on one of these tracks. I just need you to sing about two lines again.'

Cindy drained her coffee cup and stood up.

'Well, cowboy, back to the grindstone. No rest for the wicked, they say!'

Tex didn't move. Cindy glanced down at him, curious about the look he was giving her.

At length, he stared at her.

'What about you, Cindy doll? When are you gonna stop singing songs about things you ought to be saying in real life?'

Feeling the beginning of a blush on

her cheek, she tried to look puzzled.

'Come on,' he echoed her. 'You weren't singing that song about me just now. And you never did tell us who you were singing What I'd Give about!'

Cindy gave him a teasing, mysterious smile.

'Aw, don't put yourself down, Tex!'

8

The bell jangled as Hank opened the door of Lulu's. Cindy looked up from behind the bar. Her heart gave a little start, then sank again as she saw Hank's arm draped, with apparent fondness, around the shoulders of a small plump woman with shimmering long, blonde hair and a dress as yellow as a Texan cornfield.

'Hey, Cindy.' Hank grinned as he brought the woman over to the bar, 'I'd like you to meet May Chapman, your new stylist. May's gonna work on your clothes and hair for the album cover and your stage outfits.'

Cindy took the woman's plump little hand and immediately felt at ease. There was a kindly, sweet quality to May's smiley apple-cheeked face that, coupled with her roly-poly figure, reminded Cindy of Tony.

'Now, don't you worry,' May reassured her. 'I ain't gonna change ya. I'm just gonna help you pick some clothes and colours that will make you look even more beautiful than you already are.'

'May's just moved to town from Hollywood, and you couldn't name a star she hasn't dressed,' Hank explained.

Leaning on the bar, he eyed Cindy up and down.

'You know, I can't wait to get you out of that gingham waitress dress.'

Cindy gave him a coquettish smile.

'You always did have the most romantic turn of phrase, Hank.'

Hank didn't look embarrassed at being caught out admiring her figure.

'I really can't believe you're still working here.'

Tingling at the boldness of his scrutiny, but somehow not feeling flustered by it either — in fact, rather enjoying it, just as she had in the old days — Cindy lifted her chin.

'Well, I might have signed a record

deal but I don't recall seeing any money yet.'

'It'll be there as soon as the album's finished,' Hank promised. 'But you'll have to hand in your notice pretty soon, because I've finally got the sponsors and promoters in line for the tour.'

Straightening up from the bar, Hank's grey-green eyes gleamed like two ponds in the summer sun.

'We're calling it the Triple Treat Country Show!' He held up his hands as if describing blocks of neon lettering on a marquee. 'Three Great Singers — One Great Show!'

Cindy gazed up at the air where Hank's hands were. She had no trouble visualising the marquee sign for herself, and felt her heart quicken in her chest as she did so. Could it really be that it was all about to happen for her?

'Tex will go on first, because he's got the most experience,' Hank went on. 'His band's so hot after all the dates they've been doing that they'll really get the crowd worked up. You'll go on next, and towards the end of your set Tex will come back out and sing Missing You Miles with you.'

'You're gonna look wonderful up there, Cindy,' May chipped in. 'These are gonna be open-air arenas, right, Hank? I can just see you in vermillion against those azure southern skies.'

Cindy could picture it, too. She could almost feel the wind lifting her chestnut hair as she walked on to the big stage, with her microphone in her hand, the flashbulbs going off in the photographer's pit. Then the crowd stretching away into the distance, with the sun on their T-shirts, sunglasses and straw cowboy hats.

'Katie will come out for the third set,' Hank continued, 'and Tex will join her for a couple of duets. Then you'll come back out for the finale, which will be all three of you singing a couple of big finish numbers.'

Cindy pictured herself, Katie and Tex, linking hands on the front of the stage as they took their bow to a ravenous standing ovation.

'Sounds awesome!' she breathed.

'Oh, man,' Hank enthused. 'The promoters, the sponsors, the record label, the DJs . . . everybody's loving it already! We're gonna kick off in Texas, same week your album comes out, then we've got 108 straight dates all through the South. We'll take a two week break, then we've got another two months of solid shows right up the East Coast to New York. Another break, then we start out in Chicago and work our way all across the mid-west and out to Los Angeles and San Francisco.

'The whole thing will take us right up to the CMA awards, by which time I reckon you three will be just about ready to sweep the board!'

The Country Music Association Awards — country music's equivalent of the Oscars. Cindy imagined the feeling of standing in the wings as her name was called.

But, standing there in Lulu's, in her pink gingham uniform, that was just too much for her.

'Stop it, Hank!' She giggled.

'After that,' Hank was still raving 'we're already talking about another tour, starting up in the North West and heading up into Canada.'

'I said stop it! Stop it!' Laughing, Cindy closed her eyes and put her hands over her ears.

'I refuse to look that far ahead!'

Hank grinned, with his perfect white teeth.

'Well, okay,' he drawled, 'But the Triple Treat tour's as tied up as a turkey at Christmas. We've already ordered the buses. Tex wants to keep his own, but we've got two fresh from the factory. Ten-berth super buses, one each for you and Katie.'

'A bus each?' Cindy echoed in disbelief.

'You're gonna be living on 'em for nearly a year, remember,' May said.

Cindy took a moment to let the enormity of the tour sink in. Eventually, she spoke.

'Katie's gonna be pleased. A whole year without Tex going away from her, because this time they'll be on the same tour! I'll feel like a bit of a gooseberry, though.'

She had never been on tour, and she suddenly wondered what it would be like out there, roaming the endless distances between America's cities on a bus that only ever stopped moving long enough for the nightly concert. She didn't doubt that Katie and Tex would spend most of their time cosied up on the same bus, which left her cooped up on a bus to herself with just a TV for company and a band she didn't know.

The life of a country star suddenly began to look very lonely.

Her thoughts must have showed on her face, because Hank broke in.

'I'll be coming along part of the time, and May will be there. Plus, since you'll be needing a band, I figured the best guy to lead it would be the musician who understands you better than anyone in Nashville — Tony.'

Her heart leaped with joy and gratitude. Suddenly that tour bus was going to feel like home.

'You think of everything, Hank!' she said warmly. Pushing open the kitchen door with her foot, she called out.

'Hey, Tony, come out here, we've got some great news!'

Tony came through the door, beaming and wiping flour-covered hands on his apron.

'By the way,' Cindy said quickly, 'This is my new stylist May — er, Chapman, wasn't it?'

May's face, however, had frozen in shock, and when Cindy turned around, she saw that Tony's jaw had fallen open.

May finally found her voice.

'Tony . . . Kaplasky?' She shook her head, as if unable to believe her eyes.

He replied in a whisper.

'Maybeline . . . is that really you?'

9

The three tour buses and accompanying truck whooshed southwards down the highway in convoy, sunlight gleaming off their highly polished aluminium sides. In the middle bus, Cindy sat at a table just behind and to the right of the driver. She liked to be up here at the front, near the doors, where she had the most glass around her and the best view through the front and to both sides.

For five years, Cindy had turned down opportunities to go on the road as a backing singer in touring bands. The money would have been regular, but she'd preferred to take what studio sessions she could grab around town. She'd liked to stay close to the heart of the business, in the hope that one day she'd be on hand if her big break ever came — even if waiting for that break

meant spending most of her time waiting tables in Lulu's.

So gradually she'd become a town bird, happily confined to an urban village comprising East Nashville, Lower Broadway and the music industry hub of 16th and 17th Avenues.

Now, though, as the blazing sun flooded through the bus's big windows, she began to see why so many people like Willie Nelson and Tex loved to live in their buses, and why they started getting antsy if they had to spend more than a couple of nights in any bed that wasn't floating at 55mph above the tarmac!

She'd never before realised that life in perpetual motion could feel so calming. The view to the sides of the bus was a constant blurred tapestry of trees that gave way to fields, that became flyovers and industrial wastelands, cities of gleaming skyscrapers, then trees and fields again. The weather changed from burning sun to rain that splattered the glass like a carwash, then glorious blood-red sunsets and inky skies full of stars, and then pink dawns and sunshine again.

But, for all the ever-changing colours of the passing landscape, there were constants that made it seem the bus was hardly moving at all. Up ahead, through the floor to ceiling windscreen, the back of Tex's bus stayed a fixed distance away, the sun gleaming off the curve of the roof and on to the white and chrome Harley Davidson strapped to the rack on the back.

In a wing mirror the size of a dinner tray, she could see the glass and chrome front of Katie's bus, the same distance behind hers. The black ribbon of the highway with its unbroken central white line sometimes curved to the right or the left of the horizon, but its blurred colour and texture was so consistent that it gave almost no suggestion of any forward movement.

The incessant drone of the rubber tyres on the tarmac, topped off with the low purr of the passing wind, was hypnotic and reassuring. Cindy was sitting right above the wheel, and she could feel the thrumming vibration coming up through her seat and vibrating her bones at the same frequency. It made her feel connected with the road and, somehow, connected to her parents, who had lived this life before her.

At night, in her narrow bunk, with the black curtain drawn across to create a velvety cocoon, she found the unchanging note of that background hum, and the tingling vibration of the mattress deeply conducive to sleep. She knew plenty of people who couldn't sleep on a bus and came back from tours looking drained to point of collapse.

But Cindy slept more soundly and felt fresher by day than she did at home. Not having to spend the entire day on her pink high heels in Lulu's was a bonus!

Up near the ceiling behind the driver's compartment, a TV was permanently tuned to a constant stream of videos on Country Music Television. The sound was turned down to the point where it was just another layer mixed in with the background drone of the engine and the drumming of the tyres on the highway, but Cindy picked up a remote and turned it up as she saw Tex smouldering across the screen, singing his new single while standing in the bed of a beat-up pick-up truck parked in the middle of a Texan cornfield.

By coincidence, the next video was herself singing What I'd Give. It still always gave her a jolt of surprise to see herself on TV, just as it always amazed her to turn on a radio and hear her own voice coming out at her. Fascinated by the slender, graceful girl on the screen, singing her heart out in a sumptuous dress of cascading silk and flimsy net, she touched her chestnut hair and wondered if she ever looked as glamorous.

Somehow, the mental image she had of herself was still the girl in the pink gingham waitress uniform that had defined her for so long.

As the video faded out, Cindy turned the sound back down.

Hank came walking down the aisle of the bus from the little kitchenette, a mug of coffee in each hand. Cindy only just stopped herself from getting up and taking them from him. She was still getting used to the fact that she was the one who got waited on now. For the first day on the road, Hank almost had to physically restrain her from going up and down the bus taking lunch orders from the band!

Tony still did the cooking, though. He might be well on his way to becoming a rich man, having written a number one hit for Katie and co-written another chart topper for Cindy. He might sit on stage and play piano for Cindy in front of thousands of people each night.

But if one thing would have roused him to anger, even violence, it was threatening to take away his right to feed his friends roast dinners, home-made pie and pancakes. The words 'Let's hire a caterer' was fighting talk in Tony's book!

Hank sat down across the table from her. As he sipped his coffee, she watched the sun gleaming on his hair and bringing a warm glow to his face.

In that moment of sunny stillness inside the bus, as the pine trees swept by in a dark green blur outside, and the drumming of the wheels droned up through the floor, and through the soles of her sneakers and into her bones, in a way that sounded almost like soft, distant singing, Cindy doubted she had ever felt more content.

At length, she spoke.

'I guess I owe you an apology, Hank.'

He raised an eyebrow, puzzled.

'For doubting you.' She opened her hands to take in the scene as the sunshine fell through the glass of the bus.

'Here we are. A number one record in the charts. A hit album. Out on the road playing big arenas to thousands of people. Everything you ever promised me.'

Hank gave her a modest little wink and diagonal tilt of his head.

'Well, it took a long time,' he drawled. 'To tell you the truth, I had some doubts myself.'

'You never gave up, though. Looking back, I can see how hard you were working, and just how hard you have to work to even get your foot in the door in this business. Having me stop believing in you, just because the struggle seemed so hard, must have made it all the tougher for you.'

Hank gave her another slight acknowledgement. He didn't speak, but she thought she saw a slight lift of his eyebrows and a hurt look in his eyes.

Feeling guilty, Cindy went on.

'I guess I was younger then, and more impatient. I wanted everything now, and when it didn't happen I started thinking you were to blame, that maybe you were just playing at it.

Playing with me, really.'

He gave her a sympathetic look.

'I guess we've both grown up some.'

'Grown old,' Cindy joked nervously.

Hank gave her a look of the kind he used to give her all the time back in the day, the kind of look that used to melt her like toffee in a microwave.

'No,' he said, soft and low.

Getting that feeling she hadn't felt for a long, long time, Cindy looked away from him and hoped the sunshine hid the heated blush on her cheeks.

'There's one thing I promised you that hasn't ever come true,' Hank said.

Cindy felt her heart beginning to quicken. She risked a quick peek in his direction and saw he was still gazing at her with that look in his grey-green eyes. She quickly looked away again.

For a long moment, the only sound was the drone of the highway rushing by beneath them, and the thump of her own heart beating like a bass drum in her ribcage.

Slowly, he went on.

'I don't blame you for splitting up with me. I know how hard it must have been for you, hanging on for a guy like me. But when I heard you sing that song about wanting the guy back, well, I dared to wonder if there was a possibility you really felt that way about me. Because, Cindy, I sure have spent a lot of time lately, listening to that song, feeling that way about you.'

She tried to swallow, but her throat was so dry it felt like she was trying to swallow a walnut. She closed her eyes and fought the tears filling up behind her eyelids. Facing away from him, she felt a single tear escape from the corner of her lashes and begin a slow journey down the side of her face.

Hank's voice came again, barely louder than the constant background thrum of the bus.

'Do you think we could give it another go?'

She turned to him, and as she opened her eyes, the tears fell loose. She blinked twice and wiped her cheeks with the back of her hand, very aware that she was shaking her head slowly as she did so. She could hear in her head the refusal that was so ready to fall out of her mouth, but somehow she bit it back.

The truth was, she still felt an aching physical attraction to Hank, and she'd felt it all the more strongly since they'd been living on the bus. It felt strange at night, undressing for bed in the girls' compartment with Maybeline, knowing that Hank was just the other side of a black curtain with Tony and the boys in the band.

Sometimes, before she slept, as she lay with the bunk curtain drawn around her in her little cocoon, she reached back behind her pillow and touched the shiny oak-veneered partition, knowing Hank's head was just inches away on the other side. If she listened closely above the thrumming of the tyres on the road, she could hear the creak of his mattress as he turned, cleared his throat and sighed, making himself comfortable.

It was a comforting sound, and it was a comforting feeling knowing he was so close. Perhaps that was one of the reasons she slept so soundly and contentedly as the bus flew through the night.

She could understand how people had bus romances, being cooped up in such close proximity 24/7 for months at a time, the constant motion isolating them from the rest of the world.

But she didn't want a bus romance. Especially not with Hank, especially as he was her manager. How would she face him when it ended? It was bad enough now.

Probably because her parents had left her when she was so young, she'd always had a hard time with break-ups. The split with Hank had hit her harder than she would have ever believed, and she didn't want to go through it again for the sake of a fling. If she gave her heart again, she wanted it to be for keeps.

But was a bus romance all Hank was

wanting? He sounded sincere, but she knew he was more than capable of spinning a girl a line.

'I have been thinking about you a lot, Hank,' she admitted eventually.

'I'm glad. But?'

She gave a helpless little shrug.

'Going back seems kinda scary. I mean, how do you do that?'

Hank looked seriously at her, and she knew for certain he'd already been giving the question a lot of thought.

'Well, I was thinking we could just start slowly, like two people seeing each other for the first time. Take some time to get to know each other again and, you know, just kinda see if it goes anywhere.'

Cindy grinned nervously.

'Like a first date, you mean?'

Hank gave her that look again, coupled with a slight glistening in his grey-green eyes that made her feel warm inside.

'Yeah,' he drawled. 'That's exactly what I mean.'

She realised she suddenly had that heady, giggly feeling she'd first had when she fell off a kerb into his arms outside the Ryman. When that long, tall stranger with the shovel-square jaw had cracked a smile and had offered to buy her a coffee.

On that first day, he had walked her around the block to Lulu's, where he had assured her there was a guy who made the best pancakes in the whole darn world.

'Okay.' She smiled now, five years later. 'So, where are you gonna take me on our first date?'

Hank smiled with a set of perfect white teeth.

'Well, there's this little place I know, just down the bus, where the guy makes the best pancakes in the whole darn world . . . '

10

The Country Music Association Awards ceremony was the biggest night in Nashville, broadcast live to 100 million American homes from the plush surroundings of the Opryland Theatre. Everyone in the Nashville music business, from top executives to legendary stars, were in the packed and buzzing Stetson, tuxedoed and ballgowned crowd.

For once, Cindy hadn't spent all afternoon in a fluster about what to wear, because that had been planned a month in advance. Cindy and Katie both had shoulder-less, figure-hugging, floor-length dresses with a mermaid silhouette, specially made for them by the same designer. Katie's was in sparkly silver sequins that set off her cascading golden blonde curls. Cindy's was a deep purple that brought out a red and gold autumnal lustre in her chestnut brown hair.

It was a month before the awards, and Tony and Maybeline were sitting in twin catatonic states while Cindy begged Tony for the gazillionth time.

'Are you really, truly, honestly certain that this shade of purple suits me better than these other four shades of purple? Or should I start looking at blue again?'

Texan Jack wore a tuxedo suit specially tailored from black leather. He even had a black leather bow tie.

Tony beamed out of a regular tux, while Hank wore the vintage black suit of a riverboat gambler, complete with a burnished bronze waistcoat.

As Tex squared Tony's tux on his shoulders and Maybeline straightened Katie's hem in their little living room in East Nashville, Cindy looked up.

'Why don't we all go in the Chevy?' she joked.

'Because it's country music's biggest night, Cindy.'

Checking a vintage silver pocket

watch, Hank pulled aside the curtain in time to see the first in a convoy of four white stretch Hummer limousines start to fill up their little East Nashville street.

Half the neighbourhood, which almost exclusively comprised musicians, turned out on the sidewalk to see them off with whoops and hollers as the nose-to-tail limos inched forward one by one to pick up their passengers: Katie in the first, Tex in the second, Tony and Maybeline in the third and Hank squiring Cindy in the last.

The interior of the car felt vast with just the two of them in it. It was like having a bus to themselves, even if it just happened to be a bus that smelled of leather, had carpet under their feet and a mini-bar ringed with red neon!

As the limo purred along Broadway and the lights of the bars and street lamps flashed through the tinted black windows, Cindy sat bolt upright on the edge of the seat, unable to lean back because she was just too excited.

Leaning back opposite, as relaxed and composed as ever, Hank gazed at her like he could have sat gazing at her all day.

'You look beautiful,' he said, and they were the only three words either of them said during the entire journey.

Cindy just sat there smiling at him, wondering if she'd ever believe it.

At the venue, a uniformed attendant opened the door and Hank stepped out on to a red carpet. He held out his hand and Cindy took it as she gracefully inched out of the car in her floor-length gown. He crooked his elbow and she linked her arm through his.

They walked across the broad river of plush red carpet, her dress sparkled with the flashes from the photographers pressed against the velvet ropes to either side. Behind the photographers, a crush of fans cheered and called to her.

As she smiled shyly and raised one manicured hand in a small wave, she had that moment of amazement that she experienced every night when she walked on stage. As she'd learned to, she hid her doubts behind a more star-like grin.

But, walking across the red carpet, she wondered if she'd ever stop feeling like a gingham-clad waitress, carrying plates in Lulu's and checking the tables for tips. Part of her even hoped she wouldn't.

Inside, as they caught up with Tex, Katie, Tony and Maybeline, and made their way to their seats, Cindy realised she couldn't look in any direction without spotting a country music superstar.

Many of them acknowledged her with a smile or nod or, if they were closer, a handshake, a hug and peck on the cheek, as they did with Tex and Katie. Meanwhile the town's top songwriters warmly welcomed the apple-cheeked Tony into their ranks.

As always, there was a particular buzz around Dolly Parton, and when Cindy saw her, she felt a flutter in her stomach.

Slipping her arm out of Hank's, she looked up at him.

'I've just got to go over and see her.'

With several well-wishers in front of her, she was happy to hang back while admirer after admirer shook Dolly's perfectly manicured and be-ringed hand. As she watched she observed again this lady's unfailing courtesy and utter professionalism.

Before Cindy could reach the star, there was a surge of movement and the celebrity's entourage swept her off. Watching Dolly leave, she rehearsed in her mind what she'd have liked to have told her.

'There's something you won't remember, but I've got to tell you, because it meant so much to me. When I was five years old I sat on my daddy's shoulders and waited to get your autograph outside your tour bus after a show in Alabama.'

She put her head on one side, smiling at the memory.

'You were the prettiest thing I had ever seen. From that moment on, I knew what I wanted to do with my life. I wanted to be a country singer, just like you. Thank you, Dolly. Thank you from the very bottom of my heart'

* * *

The six friends all sat together — although it seemed they spent less time in their plush red seats than they did walking up to the stage to collect their awards, on the best night their little part of East Nashville had ever had!

Katie was the first called to the big shiny stage, bathed in the softly shifting pink, green and blue lights, when I Want Your Body, Cowboy picked up two awards in a row, for Single Of The Year and Music Video Of The Year. Holding the first of the hefty, Perspex, bullet-shaped awards in the air as she stepped up to the microphone to make her acceptance speech, she thanked Tony for writing it.

'My best guy friend, and the best darn songwriter in the whole of

Nashville! It's not the only number one he's written, either!' she added, with a wink at the audience, before leaving the stage.

As if to prove the truth of Katie's words, Tony was called into the spotlight for the very next award, along with Cindy and Tex, to collect the Song Of The Year award, which was presented to the three writers of Cindy's six-week chart topper, What I'd Give.

The sight of Tony and Tex each taking one of Cindy's hands to heave her out of her seat drew affectionate chuckles amid the cascading applause. But the true fact was that her legs had turned to jelly and, if Tony and Tex hadn't pulled her to her feet, she doubted she'd have been able to stand up at all!

Refusing to let go of either of their hands, she walked with them in procession all the way to the centre of the huge stage, where the female presenter was waiting, stunning in a striking emerald gown, to present them with a trophy each.

Playing up to his image as a dangerously charismatic performer, Texan Jack drew gasps from the audience when he flashed the nearest camera a switchblade grin and tossed his trophy spinning six feet into the air, then caught it one-handed, as deftly as if it were a piece of fruit.

Cindy, however, cradled her trophy as carefully as if it was a newborn baby. Glancing briefly down at it, she noticed that the hem of her dress was fluttering like a fan, she was trembling so much. Perfectly relieved to let Tony make a short acceptance speech on behalf of the three of them, she gazed out at the tiers of seats that seemed to extend in an infinite number of semi-circles from the glowing, bright blue edge of the almost mirror-topped stage.

With a semi-circle of blinding white lights glaring down into her eyes from the towering roof, everything beyond the lights was blurred into a chocolate brown haze. But even through the illusion of a thick mist, she could pick out certain individuals, all looking at her.

Dolly Parton, her heroine since she was barely a walker — the big-haired, sparkly dressed country music legend who's inspiration had started her on the journey that led her to this spot. Even Willie Nelson, one of the most successful country singers ever, was there.

Hank, of course — the man who had always promised her she'd be holding a CMA award in her hand one day. The man she had believed in and trusted so much, and whom she had gone on to distrust and reject. But who had got her here in the end, just like he said he would, and whom she had come to love again more than she loved anyone in the world.

Then there was Tony, onstage with her. He was the best friend she'd ever had. Without his insistence that she recorded What I'd Give she wouldn't have been here tonight and she couldn't have been happier about the way things were going for him and Maybeline.

Cindy couldn't even hear what he was saying, she was so overwhelmed by the emotional impact of being in the place she'd always wanted to be, surrounded by so many people whose endless love had helped her get here.

She had waited all her life, it seemed, for this one moment. Suddenly, Tony's speech was over, the theatre was ringing with applause and Tex's leather-clad arm was around her shoulders, leading her off the stage.

As Cindy returned to her seat, Katie and Hank both rose to kiss and hug her. She sat, still cradling her trophy in her lap like a baby, aware of Hank's warmth as he sat squeezed up beside her, the cosily rough wool of his vintage suit sleeve around her naked shoulders, his free hand gently caressing her forearm.

She barely registered the sight of the next couple of singers walking across the glittering stage to receive their awards for Vocal Duo Of The Year and Album Of The Year.

Then, suddenly, yet another legendary singer-songwriter was calling her name from the stage once more.

' . . . and the Female Vocalist of the Year is . . . Cindy Coin!'

She stood up in the spotlight that fell upon her, and Hank, Katie, Tex and Tony half rose to squeeze her hand in turn as she passed them. She felt herself stepping out of the bubble of sheer shock that had enclosed her until that point.

As she walked alone through the cacophonous applause, she became once more aware that this was her moment, and she was going to savour every detail in crystal clarity.

On the edge of the stage, she paused to draw a deep breath, then sashayed into the spotlight with the poise of the star she had finally become.

The presenter's large hands squeezed her shoulders and his grey beard and moustache brushed her cheek as he kissed her.

She turned to the microphone and took a deep breath.

Half her life she'd wondered what she'd say if she ever got to stand where she was now. She'd prepared a gracious speech. But, in the end, she just said it as it came out — every word flowing straight from her heart.

She thanked those country stars who had always inspired her, her friends for encouraging her, Troy for producing her records, Tony for feeding her pancakes, drying her tears and keeping her dreams alive while they worked together in Lulu's, and Katie and Tex for being the best buddies a gal could ever have.

'Finally, I want to thank a man I fell for on my very first day in town. And I mean, literally fell!' She paused to let a ripple of chuckles circle out across the auditorium. 'I was standing downtown, looking up at the Ryman with my train ticket still in my pocket and my guitar in my hand, when I slipped right off the kerb and fell into this fellow's arms. Little did I know that he'd become my manager, and the reason I'm standing here today.'

She stretched out her arm to direct the cameras to where he sat.

'Hank Donno, I love you with all my heart.'

From Alaska to Florida, households across America were treated to a close-up of a man in a 50-year-old tux, with a shovel-square jaw and smoothly oiled light brown hair as he gave Cindy a wink and tilt of his head. The faint smile that played on his lips was as unreadable as ever. To most viewers he must have looked like the coolest, least flappable guy in the world — either that, or a rabbit caught in the headlights, so shocked that he could barely twitch a muscle.

The keenest-eyed, however, might have noticed the tiniest single tear in the corner of one grey-green eye.

When Cindy got back to her seat,

carefully stepping over the trophies that she, Katie, Tex and Tony had already amassed between them, Hank half rose to hug her before she sat down.

He said something warm in her ear, but she couldn't hear it because the theatre was resounding with another blast of applause as Texan Jack Dallas was announced as Male Vocalist Of The Year.

He swaggered onto the stage in his leather tux suit, with his shirt collar ripped open and his bow tie hanging loose and undone like a scarf, looking as devilish as any man who had ever walked on to a stage, from Elvis down.

Standing loose and casual in front of the microphone he waited until the applause had abated to pin-drop silence before speaking in the deepest and sexiest of drawls.

'I guess I could thank my buddies Cindy and Tony, but those guys have taken home enough awards tonight. So, if you don't mind, I'd like to take this opportunity to say something private and deeply personal to a gal y'all know as my touring partner, but who's a lot more than that to me. Katie Carnegie. Hey, baby doll, will you marry me?'

Katie didn't hesitate. The spotlight and cameras had not even reached her when she stood up in her seat.

'Heck yes!' she hollered.

Before the final award of the night was presented, some luckless singer had to go on stage and sing a song, but Cindy doubted if anyone noticed, such were the shockwaves going through the entire audience.

Certainly nobody in their little party from East Nashville heard one single word of that song.

Once their excited exchanges of hugs, kisses and congratulations had died down, Cindy flopped back into her seat, physically and emotionally exhausted by everything that had happened.

She hugged Hank's arm.

'Wasn't that just the most romantic thing ever?'

He smiled and gave her that little wink, but at the same time he was reaching into his pocket.

'I was going to save this until later,' he drawled, 'But since I always hate to be upstaged . . . '

Cindy looked down, and saw he was holding a red velvet ring box open in his palm. Every scrap of light in the theatre seemed to glint off the diamond nestling on the scarlet satin cushion inside.

Her mouth dropping open in disbelief, Cindy realised she wasn't as emotionally drained as she'd thought! Fresh reserves of emotion flooded into her like water over Niagara Falls.

Her heart pounding, she looked up from the diamond into Hank's gleaming grey-green eyes.

'Will you marry me, Cindy Coin?' he said softly.

'Heck, yes, Hank!'

The ring fitted her finger perfectly. After admiring it on her hand for a moment, she flung her arms around his neck as he flung his around her. Their lips locked until they heard a voice on stage announcing the final and most prestigious award of the evening.

'. . . and the Entertainer Of The Year is . . . Katie Carnegie!'

Holding her award one-handed, high above her head, Katie brought the house down as she leaned towards the microphone.

'After winning three awards in one night I really think it's time for Katie Carnegie to bring her little singing career to an end. So I hope y'all have me back next year, when I'll be Katie Dallas!'

On the way home, they didn't bother with separate limos. As the fans cheered and the cameras flashed like a firework display, they spilled across the red carpet and all piled into the same Hummer.

As Hank fired a champagne cork into the mirrored ceiling and began filling glasses, Cindy held out her hand palm down to let everyone admire the diamond on her finger.

'That's beautiful,' Tony said. 'But, since I hate to be upstaged too, what do you think of this one?'

Grabbing Maybeline's left hand, he proudly displayed the engagement ring he had just bestowed on her finger.

After everyone had dished out another round of hugs, kisses and congratulations, Katie turned to Tex in a mock huff.

'Hey, after all that on stage, has somebody forgotten something here?'

She thrust her left hand in front of his face and wiggled four fingers.

'Oh, baby doll,' Tex said. 'Did I forget?'

Reaching into the deep pile of the carpet, he picked up the discarded wire cradle that had held one of the champagne corks. With a bit of pulling and pushing, he fashioned it into a circle and slipped it on to Katie's finger. 'Better now?'

Katie pouted and narrowed her eyes. 'I suppose it's the thought that counts.'

Then Tex flashed a grin, reached into his pocket and produced a velvet ring box, opening it to reveal a beautiful gem.

The laughter at Katie's expense gave way to more oohs and ahhs. But Hank, leaning forward on the leather seat, was already looking ahead.

'Now listen, you guys,' he said excitedly. 'What I'm thinking is a triple ceremony . . . on the stage of the Ryman! We'll get everybody there. It'll be bigger than tonight was. Just think of the publicity we'll get!'

Flopping back into the leather upholstery, her champagne flute in hand, Cindy watched this man admiringly.

Same old Hank, she thought, lovingly. Always talkin' about what he was gonna do.

The difference was, these days, he did it.

We do hope that you have enjoyed reading this large print book.

Did you know that all of our titles are available for purchase?

We publish a wide range of high quality large print books including:
Romances, Mysteries, Classics
General Fiction
Non Fiction and Westerns

Special interest titles available in large print are:
The Little Oxford Dictionary
Music Book, Song Book
Hymn Book, Service Book

Also available from us courtesy of Oxford University Press:
Young Readers' Dictionary
(large print edition)
Young Readers' Thesaurus
(large print edition)

For further information or a free brochure, please contact us at:
Ulverscroft Large Print Books Ltd.,
The Green, Bradgate Road, Anstey,
Leicester, LE7 7FU, England.
Tel: (00 44) **0116 236 4325**
Fax: (00 44) **0116 234 0205**